RANDY POWELL

Is Kissing a Girl Who Smokes Like Licking an Ashtray ?

A Sunburst Book
Farrar Straus Giroux

Copyright © 1992 by Randy Powell
All rights reserved
Distributed in Canada by Douglas & McIntyre Ltd.
Printed in the United States of America
First edition, 1992
Sunburst edition, 2003
1 3 5 7 9 10 8 6 4 2

Library of Congress Cataloging-in-Publication Data
Powell, Randy.
Is kissing a girl who smokes like licking an ashtray? /
Randy Powell.
    p.   cm.
Summary: An eighteen-year-old pinball addict and a smart-
mouthed girl who don't quite fit in with anyone else develop a
special relationship.
    ISBN 0-374-43628-2 (pbk.)
    [1. Interpersonal relations—Fiction.]   I. Title.

PZ7.P8778Is 1992
[Fic]—dc20

                                                    91-31062

For Judy

Is Kissing
a Girl
Who Smokes
Like Licking
an Ashtray
?

CHAPTER ONE

Biff Schmurr sat in his car halfway down the block from the girl's house, watching her front door. He had followed her straight home from school. She had just parked her car in the driveway and gone inside.

It was Friday afternoon, the first week of April. Next week was spring vacation. He wouldn't see her for nine days, unless he hung around the supermarket where she bagged groceries, or unless he asked her out.

He had been in love with her for twenty-three months. Ever since May of his sophomore year, when he'd first seen her walking down the hall in shorts and blue-and-white-striped knee socks. He still hadn't been able to say anything more than "Hi" to her, or sometimes "Hi, Tommie." (Her name was Tomassa Isaac; she went by Tommie.) He estimated that he had driven by her house 184 times. He knew her classes, her activities, her routes to and from school and work. He thought of her constantly. He dreamed of her, awake and asleep.

In his spare time he'd been trying to write a poem about her, backward. It went:

> *Slegn a nise veil eboh weimmot*
> *Won snig river up*

which, forward, was "Tommie who believes in angels / Pure virgin snow."

That was all he had so far. He wasn't much of a poet, backward or forward.

He'd ask her out soon, though; maybe even next week. He just needed a little more time to come up with a plan. He was going on a hike tomorrow, to do some thinking and strategizing, to figure out how he was going to approach her.

But the hike needed planning, too. After all, he was no more a hiker than he was a poet; he couldn't just go crashing off into the wilderness. Not if it was to be the kind of experience he hoped it would be. No, he had to come up with the perfect hike. Something spectacular. Something, most importantly, devoid of other humans. Only then would the hike help restore his soul and raise his consciousness to a higher plane, where he might glimpse a couple of the great Truths of Life—as well as figure out what to do about Tommie Isaac.

Biff noticed he was gripping the steering wheel and his knuckles were turning white. This was not good. He opened his hands and wiggled his fingers to bring back the circulation.

The past couple of months, things had been getting to him. The same old irritations mostly—the ones he thought he had learned to live with. He'd recently turned eighteen but he looked fourteen; his whole adolescent life, he'd always looked four years younger than whatever age he was. He hated that. Then there was his weird, uncontrollable hair: thick, wavy, unruly, sprouting out of his head in all directions, like a shrub, a great tuft of weeds. And he had been cursed with extremely pale, tender skin, and a set of clownishly red cheeks and lips. He had no friends, except Ray Hu, a mere ninth-grader, but a good guy and a decent chess player. And now another spring was here and he'd never had a girlfriend, never kissed a girl, could not even talk to a girl without freezing up.

Still, with Tommie Isaac, there might be some hope. After twenty-three months, things seemed to be coming to a head. Six times last month she had said "Hi, Biff" in the hallway, instead of just "Hi," and twice she had actually said "Hi" *before* he did.

And then, just last Friday, the Major Development. Maybe the high point of his life.

He had written an essay for English called "Some Thoughts on Love." (Of course, he had secretly dedicated it to Tommie.) His English teacher had liked it so much she read it to her other English classes. That Friday afternoon—Good Friday, actually, coming into Easter weekend—he'd closed his locker door and turned to find Tommie Isaac standing there, looking at him—or, rather, at his right hip—with an awkward, shy smile. "Hi, Biff," she had said. "I—I just wanted to—Mrs. Henderson read us your—that essay you wrote? It was really—I really liked it."

Biff had been thunderstruck—unable to form a word, not even a "thanks." Locker doors were banging shut all around them. Tommie shrugged and their eyes met for a second. "Well," she said, "I just—you know—wanted to tell you that." And then she smiled, looked down, hesitated, turned, bumped into a passerby, and walked away.

This past week, he'd been careful not to force anything. He thought it best to lie low for a time and stay out of her way. Mustn't haunt her. Be patient. Don't rush into anything.

But why had he tailed her this afternoon? That was risky; there was always the chance she'd spot him lurking and think he was a pervert. Why was he parked down the block from her house this afternoon, staring at her front porch and her pink front door? Maybe he *wanted* to force something? He pictured himself getting out of his car and walking up to her door and knocking and— ho boy! Imagine it! But why not? Why did he need to think and plan anymore? Wasn't twenty-three months enough?

Biff now realized he was biting down on his lower lip. He leaned back and opened and closed his mouth. His jaw cracked. He should have gone up to her the first time he ever saw her in the hall at school. But why *not* right now? Such a simple solution. Or maybe he should go home and call her. Yes, calling her might be better. You don't just go up to a girl's door and pound on it like you're making a drug bust. Catch them without their makeup on and you're dead—they'll never be able to face you again.

Yes, calling her was probably best. But not tonight. That would seem overeager and obvious, what with spring vacation here; it implies you're chomping at the bit. Besides, she usually worked Friday and Saturday nights at the supermarket. No, he'd stick to his original plan: Up early tomorrow morning, drive somewhere out into nature for an all-day hike, come home rejuvenated and inspired, call her Sunday or Monday evening. Or Tuesday.

Good plan. Subject, of course, to revision during the hike.

The hike. The all-important hike. Where to go, that was the question. For days he'd been hunting for his copy of *47 Secret Hikes in the Olympic Mountains*. He'd bought it a long time ago at a garage sale, but had never read it. Finding that book had now become an obsession. He'd looked everywhere, but with no luck.

Now, on a sudden impulse, he dove down on the floor of his car and began rummaging through the debris and rubble. It *had* to be here. He found three books, a quarter, two Teeny Bouncers, two soiled white wristbands, several pennies, three pens, a half-empty bag of french fries, a Phillips screwdriver, and a slip of paper with an unknown address on it. But no *47 Secret Hikes*. The wristbands— whose were they? Biff had never worn a wristband in his life. They must have belonged to—

Aha! He remembered. He knew where the book was.

He'd lent it, months ago, to Pam and Lynn Kobleska.

Pam and Lynn were a married couple in their mid-twenties. They were both good friends of Biff's family, especially of his sister, Willa. In fact, it was Willa who had brought Pam and Lynn together and had helped get them back together the time they'd split up a couple of years back.

Laughing out loud with relief, Biff pulled himself up off the floor, started his car, and took off.

CHAPTER TWO

The Kobleskas' condo was thirteen miles away, just west of the Ballard district in Seattle, on the edge of Puget Sound. Biff had to stop his car at the security gate and tell the guard who he was visiting. He didn't know why they bothered having a security guard at this place; all they ever did was stand in the booth and watch old movies on the portable TV. After being waved through, Biff pulled into a space marked GUEST.

On his way to the lobby, he took a Teeny Bouncer out of his pocket and threw it, underhanded, high into the blue sky, watched it dive down spinning to earth, and caught it in his right hand, without breaking stride.

These firm superballs, the size of a pinball or an eyeball or the inner core of a golf ball, with swirling colors of blue, orange, and yellow, and TAIWAN in tiny raised letters that he could feel with his fingertips—these superballs were a kind of therapy for him.

Biff was a pinball addict. Whenever he walked by a pinball machine, his hand would automatically slide into his pocket for a quarter. During the past few months, he had gotten especially hooked on one particular machine called Buildup, at the Earl of Nottingham Lanes. Lately he'd been trying to reach for a Teeny Bouncer instead of a quarter, and so far, it was working: he'd been pinball-free for twelve days.

Biff tossed the Teeny Bouncer up higher than before and—amazingly—missed. It nicked the side of his hand and bounced merrily into the landscaped azaleas. He hustled after it.

"Hey, you! Hey, young fella! Get outa them bushes! You know better 'n that. Hey!"

Old man Follett, the manager. The old coot. Biff, down in the bark dust on all fours, pretended not to hear him.

"Hey now, out! You heard me! Get outa there before I call Security!"

Biff stood up, brushing the bark dust off his pants but not moving from his spot. Follett, in green coveralls, hobbled toward him.

"I was just looking for my . . ."

"Hah? You're not supposed to go in there. Get out!"

Shaking his head, Biff came out obediently, back onto the walkway, feeling like a kid. Like a lousy little kid. Search & Rescue aborted, another Teeny Bouncer declared MIA. Bad luck. You're eighteen, Schmurr, he scolded himself. Tell this geezer to shove it.

"I—I wasn't . . ."

"Hah? Yeah, yeah, yeah." Follett, holding a nonfilter

cigarette between two stubby fingers, continued to wave Biff toward the front door of the lobby. "You ain't even a resident here. Who's it you visit here, ennaways? Kobleskas, ain't it?"

Biff was about to answer but was interrupted by the sight of a girl coming toward them up the walkway. She had pretty blond hair and a creamy complexion, and was wearing what Biff thought was an interesting jacket, a blue seaman's navy jacket, with big buttons that had anchors on them.

"Afternoon, there, miss." Follett gave her a suspicious nod while holding the door open for her.

Biff couldn't guess how old she was, but there was something young about her, and stunning.

The girl hesitated before entering the lobby.

"I don't suppose you'd give me a cigarette," she said to Follett, without bothering to look at him. She didn't sound rude, just certain he'd turn her down, which of course he did, and not pleasantly.

She turned to Biff. "I don't suppose you even . . . No." She shook her head and walked through the door that Follett was still holding open. Biff caught her breeze. Girls' breezes were one of the blessings of life. Tommie's breeze carried in it the main floor of a department store. This girl's breeze gave off the scent of green apples— probably her shampoo.

Biff and Follett watched her wait for the elevator.

"She live here?" Biff asked.

"Hah? Nah. Just visiting for a few days. Somebody's niece." Follett scratched the white stubble on his head with his stumpy fingers. "Now, whose niece . . . ?" Scratch scratch. "I'll be a duck . . ." He flicked his cigarette into the landscaped bark dust, where it sat burning. "You know? I'll be a duck if she ain't the Kobleskas' niece?"

"Huh," was all Biff said as he watched the girl disappear behind the elevator's two silver doors.

CHAPTER THREE

Biff left Follett (who didn't hold the door open for him) and passed through the lobby and into the elevator, where the scent of green-apple shampoo still lingered. The Kobleskas' niece? Could be. Pam had a niece, didn't she? What was her silly name —Happy? Wendy? Wendy sounded right. Or no . . . Heidi? He'd never liked that name, *Heidi*. It reminded him of a fat cherry-cheeked Fräulein serving beer and sausages in some beer hall to a group of drunk singing German soldiers who swatted her on her huge rear end. Biff shook his head. Jeesh. Bumming cigarettes off the manager. You've got to wonder about girls who smoke. Who was it who once said, "Kissing a girl who smokes is like licking an ashtray"?

The elevator doors opened to a fifteenth-floor view of Puget Sound and the Olympic Mountains. He walked down the hall and lingered in front of the Kobleskas' door before knocking.

Pam answered.

"Biffy! I was just thinking about you! I mean that! I know I say that to everybody, but this time it's for real. I called you twice this afternoon. How dare you not be home." She pulled Biff into the living room.

He explained about the book while Pam handed him a can of diet cream soda. Everything was diet at Pam's, even though she was skinny and not even five feet tall. Pert and perky Pam. She had brown hair which she flipped up just above her shoulders—Mary Tyler Moore, circa 1965.

"I need it for this weekend," Biff said.

"Need what?"

"The book."

"Oh, Biffy, you don't hike. You drive."

"Yeah, but I—I thought I'd . . ." He looked down at the white carpet.

"Aren't you even going to guess why I've been trying to get hold of you?" she asked.

"Uhh . . ."

"I want you to come to dinner. Not tonight, though. I don't have any food. But I want you to meet somebody."

"Your niece?"

"You weren't supposed to guess! Now you'll probably chicken out. What'd you do, meet her in the lobby?"

"I think so."

"Smoking her last-minute cigarette, no doubt."

"I kind of forgot you had a niece."

"Biffy, I have three."

"Oh."

"She came in a few nights ago," Pam said. "Her visit was just a *tad* bit unexpected."

"She on spring vacation?"

"Oh, no, Spokane had theirs back in March. No, she kind of got—what's the word?—kicked out. For a while."

"Suspended?"

"Yeah, suspended."

Biff cracked a smile. "She light up in the lavatory or something?"

"Or something."

Pam's kettle whistled and she went after it, leaving Biff to admire the picture-window view of the Olympics. Tomorrow he'd be over there somewhere, a solitary hiking speck. But the book . . . He had to find the book. Lynn must know where it was.

"Where's Lynn, by the way?" he asked Pam, who'd returned with a cup of tea.

"Studying at the law library, as usual. What'd you think of her?"

"Who?"

"My niece."

"Your niece."

"Yeah."

"Well I . . ." Biff cleared his throat. "She was wearing an interesting coat."

"That navy thing? It smells like cigarettes. Biffy, where've you been hiding lately? Lynn and I have missed you. What have you been up to these days?"

"Oh, well I—"

"Biff, what's that all over your pants?"

"Hm?—bark dust."

"I despise bark dust. Did we pick a night?"

15

"No." He took a swig of diet cream soda and burped with his mouth closed. "Uh . . . a night for what?"

"Dinner, silly. I tried to make it to the store today, but Heidi and I ended up visiting art galleries instead."

Something orange streaked across the living room. It was the Kobleskas' cat, Thermal.

"You think he'll be home soon?" Biff asked.

"Who, Lynn? Stop asking about him. You'll make me think you came to see him instead of me."

Biff muttered something about the book. He was beginning to worry they didn't have it.

"Ask me something about me," Pam said, which Biff promptly did, allowing him time to think. Hadn't Lynn borrowed the book? It must be here somewhere. Probably in Lynn's study. But what if he couldn't find it? Well, there was always the Wallace Falls trail. Or Mt. Si—

Pam was describing her latest artistic endeavors. The tactile and emotive aspects of blah blah.

"Oh! Biffy! Guess what else. Guess what I'm doing. Go on, guess."

Biff took a guess.

"No, no, I'm doing volunteer work. You know, a thousand points of light and all that? At the Seattle Art Museum. You've been there, of course."

"Not for years," Biff said. "I used to climb on the stone lions out front."

"Well, I'm a docent. I get all dressed up in smart skirts and blouses and business suits, and I take little groups of people around and explain the art to them, and I have to shout at the senior citizens and find places for them to sit, but the children, Biffy, they're wonderful, so inquisitive and—hey, Biffy?"

"What?"

16

"Want to meet my niece?"

He looked around the living room and cleared his throat, then looked back at Pam. "Uh, sure."

"She's a good kid. A teeny bit on the wild side, if you know what I mean, but you'll like her."

Biff nodded, even though he had no idea what people meant by *wild*. It conjured up an image of girls in black tights, cutoff T-shirts, exposed belly buttons, hanging around outside the video arcade, cigarette dangling from their pouty red lips.

This thought gave him a slight tremor. He quickly apologized to Tommie Isaac.

"You mean, uh, rebellious?" he said out loud.

Pam laughed. "Your voice sounded funny. Rebellious? A little, I guess. Not like her mother was, though. And she's got more smarts than Kim ever had. Don't let her fool you into thinking she's a dummy. She'll try. She tries to hide her intelligence, for some reason. And she makes me feel so old, Biffy! Like such an old aunt. What a smart-mouthed brat she can be! Which I personally find stimulating, in small doses, but Gary and Sherri can't seem to handle."

"Gary and Sherri? She lives with your brother's family?"

"Yeah, ever since Kim died. It's been seven years. Actually, she lived with my mother the first two years, and Gary and Sherri the last five. She's almost sixteen now. Sweet sixteen. This isn't the first time she's gotten herself into a mess at school. It's that smart mouth of hers."

"Why's she here?"

"Good question. Something's going on, but Lynn and I aren't sure what. I guess, hmmm . . . I guess everyone needed to call a cease-fire. Gary was ready to wring her neck. So we said we'd take her for the rest of her what-chamacallit. Suspension. Although we didn't have much of a choice, considering she was already on the train and halfway here by the time we found out about it. That train, you know? It was two hours late! I had to go by myself because Lynn, of course, was studying. Have you ever picked someone up at King Street Station in the dead of night? Yik. So anyway, she's here until next Friday. Then we ship her back on the train to Spokane. She'll have to face the music. And if she blows it this time, Gary's going to sell her into slavery or something."

"One more question," Biff said.

"Wait a sec." Pam took a final gulp of tea. "Okay. Ask."

"Your sister Kim was married, right?"

"To Marc Hamilton, yes."

"Then why doesn't your niece . . . Why didn't her father . . . ?"

"Why didn't he take his daughter?" Pam looked over her shoulder toward the bedrooms, then back to Biff, and lowered her voice. "Oh, God, Biff. That's a can of worms." She made a face. "Her father's a mess. A god-awful mess. Wait here. Let me go see if I can drag her out of her cave."

CHAPTER FOUR

Biff fell back on the couch after Pam had started down the hall toward the bedrooms. She tended to wear him out. He watched her white pants recede into the shadows, then turned and looked out the window at a freighter heading north up the Sound. In the background, the Olympics looked blue and faint. Clouds were gathering on the horizon.

The book . . . He stood up and began scanning the titles on the shelves in the living room, but they were all those huge art books nobody reads. He stopped and looked around. Pam and Lynn's condo was much more elegant than you'd expect a young married couple—an artist and a law student—to own. Plush white carpet. Abstract paintings. Pam's gnarled, inexplicable wooden sculptures. Over the fireplace hung a large framed photo of Lynn and Pam on their wedding day, the five grooms-men and bridesmaids flanking them like a V, a flying football wedge. Biff's sister, Willa, maid of honor, stood beside Pam. Pale spindly Willa had looked pretty that day.

Biff remembered the wedding, four years ago, over in Spokane. He'd been fourteen at the time and Willa twenty-two; they'd driven over together. As weddings went, it had been tolerable: short ceremony, no praying or embarrassing speeches by the groom or bride, a sound-proof nursery for screaming infants. And the outdoor reception—good grief! Smoked salmon, fresh crab, oysters, clams, mussels, corn on the cob, a pig revolving over a pit of coals. For their wedding present, Pam's mother had given them this condo, bought it outright and laid it in their laps—a *condo*! Right on Puget Sound! How disgusted Willa had been. "Don't you see? It's so obvious. She's already poking her nose in their lives from day one. Deciding where they're going to live. Controlling them, *buying* them. The old biddy."

He remembered meeting the old biddy at the reception and being terrified of her. She'd had so many face-lifts her face was permanently frozen into a grisly, startled sneer. She'd been married several times herself, each husband richer and nearer to the grave than the last, and she'd given her children—Kim, Gary, and Pam—an exotic, cushy life. Especially Pam. Willa and Pam had first met at summer camp in eastern Washington when they were both thirteen. They had stayed best friends all these years, even though Pam had grown up in Spokane and Willa in Seattle.

Biff didn't remember meeting any nieces at the wedding. Certainly not that blond Heidi, who would have been what, eleven? Her mother, Kim, would have been three years dead. Maybe Heidi was too "wild" even back then to be allowed out in public.

A mess. What had Pam meant by calling Marc Hamilton that? Biff had never met him, but he'd heard things from Willa. He was a failed or floundering writer who had written only one book, *Morning Fog* or *Fog in the Morning* or something, which had been made into a movie. Biff decided he'd have to pump Willa for more information.

Pam had been gone a long time. Biff sat on the sofa with his head resting against the back, looking at a series of oval shadows on the ceiling that, after a few minutes, he realized were his own head. He glanced at his watch: 4:52. Why drag the poor girl out if she didn't want to come? Sometimes Pam was so much like his sister it was downright scary. This had all the makings of an Awkward Situation. Like when Willa made him meet people. Why did you have to go through life being forced to do things like meet new people? Maybe he should just sneak away, flee to the mountains right now, forget about the book.

He stood up.

A door opened. Footsteps. He sat back down on the sofa and crossed his legs but uncrossed them at the last second.

"Here we are!" Pam's voice sounded a bit strained. "Biffy, may I present my niece, Heidi. My niece Heidi, this is my very own Biff."

"Gary and Sherri's next-door neighbors have a dog named Biff," the niece said.

"I hear that quite often," Biff said.

Pam laughed. "What do you mean, you hear that! You couldn't have heard that."

"No, I guess not," Biff said, looking down. "I meant, it's a common name. For a dog."

Awkward silence.

"Biff is eighteen," Pam said, looking at him as though she were explaining one of her sculptures—one that hadn't turned out quite right. "I just thought we should clarify that."

The niece looked at him. "Pam says you admired my navy coat. I suppose you tattled on me and told her I was trying to bum a cigarette off the manager."

"I—huh?" Startled, Biff shook his head no. His face was hot.

"Why do you go 'bumming' for things?" Pam said to her niece. "And from the manager, for goodness' sake. As if he'd give you one. And he smokes those awful nonfilters."

"He gave me one yesterday."

"He did not, you liar."

"Without knowing it, he did. He left his pack on that table in the lobby where he sits and plays solitaire. I peached a couple from him. That's a word, isn't it? To peach something?"

Biff, rising to the occasion, knew the answer to this. He knew. Let's see . . . peach . . . to peach . . .

"You boast about stealing . . ." Pam was saying to her niece.

"It's not exactly the—not exactly the right use of the verb *to peach*," Biff said, but it was too late. They weren't paying any attention.

". . . to support a lethal, unclean habit," Pam went on.

"Everything's lethal," the niece said.

"Reminds me of a . . ." Biff chuckled. He suddenly

decided he'd try to loosen up. Forget about the verb *to peach*. "By the way, uh,"—he raised his voice—"you guys know what they say about—uh—kissing—uh—kissing a girl who smokes is lick—like . . ." His voice trailed off feebly, pathetically. They were ignoring him; he was talking to himself, to no one.

". . . I can't help it if I happen to smoke," the niece was saying.

"Oh, you goose," Pam said, "you're not addicted. As much as you'd like to think you are."

"We're all going to die someday," Heidi said, inspecting her glossy fingernails.

"Let's drop it," Pam said.

"Oh, do let's!" Heidi said in a snotty voice.

"Be civil while Biff is here," Pam said crisply, "and don't use that particular tone."

"She's always talking about particular tones and being civil." Biff found himself being addressed by the niece. "Like I'm some kind of raging beast. Like all that matters is being civil."

"It helps, dearie," Pam said.

"Ci-vil. I hate that word. It's so Gary. Snaky and slithery, like Gary the Snake."

"Oh, God." Pam rolled her eyes.

"I'm tired of this conversation," Heidi said, sighing. "Can I go back to my room now?"

"Fine with me," Biff muttered.

Slowly, Heidi's head rotated to him. "Excuse me? Did you say something?" Her eyes looked him up and down. Biff wondered if this was what they called a withering glance. He did feel a little withered.

"Is there some reason why you wanted me to meet

him?" Heidi asked her aunt, keeping her eyes on Biff.

"My goodness, you *are* a raging beast," Pam said. "Not a trace of manners."

"Another Gary word," Heidi said, finally looking away from Biff. "Manners. Another word for bullshit."

"She's going through this phase where she thinks she can shock people with her dirty mouth," Pam explained to Biff. "Lynn says most kids go through it in about seventh grade. She's a late bloomer."

"Like Lynn's an expert or something," Heidi said, rolling her eyes. "But at least he sort of *approaches* cool. I wonder why he married you?"

Pam gave her niece a sugary smile. "Isn't she just the sweetest thing? I don't know why I'm so crazy about her. Come here, you"—taking Heidi's face in her hands and squeezing it—"I don't know why I'm so crazy about you, you sweet thing."

The niece almost smiled despite the two red pinch-marks her aunt's fingers had left on her cheeks. "I was thinking I might go to the library and get more books. Do you think he"—Biff now saw himself being pointed at—"might give me a ride?"

"You just went two nights ago," Pam said. "And why don't you ask *him*."

There followed a rapid-fire exchange between aunt and niece about whether any branch libraries were open past six on Friday nights. Biff gave up trying to follow it. He snuck a look at his watch. What time should he set his alarm for tomorrow? Maybe he should have Willa wake him up before she went to her archery lesson? Maybe he should just do the Wallace Falls hike? No, it wasn't long enough and the name reminded him of his brother, Wallace Jr. Besides, it would be swarming with people. Same with Mt. Si. He wanted some place new and a little more green and meadowy. Like England or something. Verdant—yes, that was the word. *Verdant.*

"I'll just get my coat," Heidi said and then turned to Biff. "The one you admired."

"He hasn't said he's *leaving* yet," Pam said. "He just *got* here. And you haven't asked him."

"I'll just hold on to it until he leaves, and follow him out. Is that bad manners?"

She headed toward the front closet.

Pam winked at Biff. "Well, what do you think? Smart as a whip or what?"

Biff again mentioned the book. Pam went away and came back with another diet cream soda for Biff, who, opening it, marveled at how diet cream soda could taste so bad when regular cream soda tasted so good.

Heidi returned carrying her coat under her arm.

"Your closet smells like celery," she said to Pam.

"Your coat smells like cigarettes," Pam said.

"So?"

"So? Do you want all your clothes to smell like cigarettes?"

"Yes."

"How are you getting home?"

"Bus."

"Call. I'll come pick you up. Or Lynn will."

Bratty look: "Yes, Aunt Pam."

"Biff, can I get you another cream soda?"

He looked at his full can. "I uh—you just—"

The phone rang. Pam went off to answer it. Heidi and Biff were left alone.

He looked at her.

"Which, uh . . ."

"What?" she said, putting her coat down. "I can't hear you."

"I was wondering which, uh . . . library you were going to."

"Do you think this looks better tucked in or untucked?" she said, ignoring his question. She was pulling at her black thin sweater. She showed him both versions.

This, thought Biff, is a first.

"Well?" she said. "Which do you think? In or out?"

"Show me tucked in again."

She unsnapped her pants and tucked it in.

"I—uh—like it like that," he said. "Tucked in."

"You would." She untucked it.

He looked around the living room and cleared his throat and spoke up. "Which, uh . . . branch library did you say . . . ?"

Again, she simply ignored him. It dawned on him that she had no intention of going to any library.

"Well, that was Lynn," Pam said, returning. "He says Hi, Biff, and he's going to be late and dinner for tomorrow night is fine. And late—the later the better. That's very East Coast. I hate eating early on Saturday night. So we all like late Saturday best, right? You're not booked up tomorrow night, are you, Biff?"

Biff looked down at his tennis shoes, muttering something about a hike. No one, not even he, listened. His eyes traveled along the white carpet and came to the girl's shoes, her ankles, her pants. He decided the black sweater looked as good untucked as tucked. She had a slim, sporty figure. No baby fat, like Tommie. Her new white tennis shoes were petite. Her legs and hips were skinny—unlike Tommie's, which were rather wide—and her tight black pants came up above her bare ankles, one of which had a silver bracelet around it that gave Biff's heart a thump.

Meanwhile, Heidi was looking at him. "I was wrong about his cheeks being red," she said to Pam. "They're more of a . . . almost a magenta. But we really should be going," she said.

"Oh, but he just got here!" Pam said. "Well, listen, Biffy"—she clapped her hands once—"I'm so glad you came—and that, Heidi, is not just good manners. And I'll let you know immediately if and when I find that hiking book—that *is* just good manners. Biff, I know you don't like comments about your appearance—he says his sister does it too much—but senior year is definitely agreeing with you. That was a weird thing to say, wasn't it? What an auntish thing to say. 'Senior year is agreeing with you.' It's having this niece here. She makes me feel old and prissy."

"You are old and prissy," the niece said.

"Come around eightish, Biffy. That'll give you plenty of time to goof off all day. You're not booked up, are you?"

Biff had to concede that he was not booked up for dinner.

"Maybe Heidi will cook it," Pam said.

Biff rubbed his eye and said maybe he was booked up after all. It got a laugh from Pam. Heidi looked at him, shook her head, and said, "What an irritant."

"Believe it or not, she's a good little cook, aren't you, Heiders."

"You just sounded so much like Gary the Snake I think I'm going to run away," Heidi said. She put on her navy coat but didn't button it, then grabbed a lumpy black carry bag.

Pam gave her niece a peck on the cheek—"Bye, brat"—and Biff a quick hug, and Biff realized he was being swept out the door. "I guess I'd better be going," he said, halfway into the hall.

The door closed and he and this apple-scented tart were walking down the hall together to the elevator. Dazed and confused, Biff had a sudden desire to play pinball. Oh, Buildup, yes, that was what he needed. It had been a mistake to come here.

He should have fled into the mountains when he had the chance.

CHAPTER FIVE

In his car, Biff knocked a few hamburger wrappers and napkins on the floor to clear a place for Heidi's rump. It was another first: a girl in his car. (Willa didn't count.)

"Which library?" he asked for the third time.

"You really have a thing about that, don't you?"

"Well, I just—I'd just kind of like to know which direction I'm supposed to go."

"Don't get huffy," Heidi said.

"You're not even going to the library," he muttered.

She half turned to face him. "Uh, I beg your pardon? What did you say? Like, are you calling me a liar? Thank you."

Okay. He wouldn't ask again. He'd drive until his car ran out of gas.

He turned out of the parking lot and drove slowly along

the boulevard, with the Sound on the left and the high wooded bluff on the right. Out of the corner of his eye he noticed that the girl was fishing in her pocket for something. A stray cigarette? If she tried to light up in his car, he'd . . .

She did find something. A piece of bubble gum. She tore the wrapper off and popped it into her mouth, reading the comic while taking the first hard chews.

"Ha ha," she said. She handed it to him, pointing at the slogan in black letters below the comic. Sometimes there was a riddle or fortune, sometimes just an unfunny saying of some sort. Biff slowed down and noticed how long and slender her fingers were, each with at least one silver ring. He found what she was pointing at and read: DON'T ACCEPT RIDES FROM THREE-LEGGED CAMELS.

He gave her a side glance, not even able to muster a polite chuckle.

She was now leaning forward, reaching under her rear end, feeling around, as though sitting on something uncomfortable, and she eventually came up with one of his Teeny Bouncers. Meanwhile, Biff had turned right and they were heading up the steep, winding road which took them away from the Sound, to the main arterial. Heidi dribbled his Teeny Bouncer against the dusty dashboard. Her bracelets, sliding up and down her forearm, jangled. Biff was impressed. She had a degree of Teeny Bouncer finesse. Her hand-wrist action was fluid.

"Are you Canadian?" she asked in a rather loud voice, still bouncing the ball.

"What? No."

They drove along for a few minutes in silence.

"Why?" he asked. "Why did you ask that?"

"Relax, would you?"

He sped up, then slowed down. He scratched the back of his head with a sudden vigorous doglike motion.

"You—you must have had a reason."

"God!" she said, laughing. "Don't have a tizzy."

"You don't—you don't just go asking somebody if they're . . ." He shook his head.

He slowed down at a four-way stop. "Oh, by the way," he said loudly, "are you Portuguese?"

"Yeah, right." She rolled her eyes.

"I mean, I was just wondering, you know? No *reason*."

"What is your problem?" she said. "Pull over up there, would you?"

"Huh?"

"Pull over there, that store. I want some cigarettes."

"Oh brother."

He pulled over to the curb in front of a mom-and-pop grocery store that had black bars on the door and windows, and a Coke sign out front with the name of the store in black letters: Lucky 4 U.

"Will you buy them for me?" she asked.

"What?"

"You have to be eighteen."

"Oh boy, oh boy," he muttered, shaking his head. He held out his hand without looking at her.

"I'll pay you tomorrow," she said. "I forgot my money."

He looked at her for a second, then withdrew his hand and started to get out of the car.

"Now," she said.

He stopped and gave her another look. "No, I thought I'd wait till next Thurs—"

"No, that's the brand I want!" she said, laughing. "Now. Regular, not menthol."

A fat old man displaying several chins and wearing a green apron sat behind the counter reading the newspaper. Biff put his last three crumpled dollars on the counter and waited for him to look up from the paper. Here's a man, Biff thought, who has found his one true calling: to own a little neighborhood store, to wear that apron, to sit behind the counter reading the newspaper after he had swept the sidewalk, to sell candy to kids after school for nickels and dimes. Hm, thought Biff. A rather profound observation.

Biff cleared his throat. "Uh . . ."

The man licked his finger and turned a page of the newspaper.

Biff cleared his throat again. "Uh—pack of Nows?"

Finally looking up: "You eighteen?"

"Huh? Yeah."

"Prove it."

Biff reached into his back pocket for his wallet. His fingers were flushed and trembling. Here we go, another geezer. Why did he always seem to find the ones that raised his hackles? He put his driver's license on the counter, somehow feeling guilty and dishonest. The old man picked it up and squinted at it with his mouth open, breathing noisily.

"That don't look like you."

"It's me."

"You look about fourteen."

The man tossed the license on the counter and began a slow, methodical combing of the shelves.

"I see them right there," Biff said, pointing.

The man ignored him. Eventually he found them on his own, tossed them on the counter, opened the cash register, took the three crumpled bills, slowly smoothed each one, and plunked down the change.

"You look fourteen," the man said.

"You already said that," Biff said, feeling his right eye begin to twitch.

"Yeah? I'll say it again. You look fourteen."

"You look eighty-eight!" Biff said.

"Touchy, aren't we? Have fun smoking your cancer sticks there, cowboy."

"You have a nice day, too, mister. You—you have yourself a nice day."

"Chop suey, pal."

Biff walked back to his car, fuming. He threw the cigarettes on Heidi's lap.

"What's the matter with you?" she asked.

"Chop suey!" He kept looking back at the store. "What a dick! Just a guy with a king-size chip on his shoulder or something. Why do I always get 'em? Sheesh!"

Biff gripped the steering wheel and closed his eyes for a few seconds. Why did he let people push his buttons? Did he *ask* for it? Why couldn't he be a "people person" like his sister, Willa?

Taking a few deep breaths, he gained control of himself and started the car but stayed idling for a minute. He looked over at the girl. A girl was sitting in his car opening a pack of cigarettes. She didn't seem to be trying to escape.

Relax, he told himself. Think of something clever, something a people person might say.

"Who was it . . ." He stopped and cleared his throat. "I wonder who it was who once said, 'Kissing a girl who smokes is like licking an ashtray.' "

She showed no reaction. Did not bat an eyelash. "I think it was that President," she said.

Biff blinked. "Who?"

"That President."

"The Canadian one, no doubt," he said, shaking his head.

"No, the crippled one. With the initials."

He stared. "Initials."

"Yes."

"F.D.R.? You mean Franklin Delano Roosevelt?"

"Yes. I believe he said it."

Biff rubbed his face. "I—I don't think he said that. I think he said, 'We have nothing to fear but fear itself.' But I don't think he said that."

"I don't suppose you bothered to get matches."

"Correct."

"This'll do." She pushed in the lighter on the dashboard.

He pulled away from the curb. What an incredible airhead. The first official girl to enter his car was an official airhead.

He turned down a side street to get away from a jerk riding his rear end. He hated people who rode him for driving too slow. The lighter popped out and Heidi, tossing her gum out the window, lit her Now. With no destination, Biff turned down one side street after another to avoid traffic, those tailgating jerks, and flipped up and down the FM dial.

He glanced at Heidi, who was puffing away contentedly.

"I think it was a stand-up comic," he said.

"Who cares," she said, releasing a cloud of smoke. "It wasn't funny."

"About as funny as three-legged camels," Biff said. "Could you crack your window open?"

"Oh, God."

Biff suddenly realized he was going the wrong way down a one-way street. He pulled into someone's driveway to turn around and was met by a huge dog bounding up and barking hysterically, and Heidi said "Oops." Of all the incredibly airhead things to say. *Oops.* Tommie Isaac, out of pure tact, wouldn't have said anything; would have pretended not to notice. Tommie Isaac wouldn't have *had* to pretend, because Biff wouldn't have done something like that with her in the car, because he wouldn't have had to stop to buy cigarettes. But even if she'd noticed, she wouldn't have said "Oops."

He would just drive home. Let Heidi sit in the driveway all night if she wanted to, he was going to go home, get up early tomorrow morning, and head for the mountains. Forget the stupid book, it had been a mistake to go after it. He knew it had been bad luck to lose that Teeny Bouncer in front of the condo.

"Want to see a picture of my boyfriend?" the airhead asked.

"No."

She unzipped her black bag and extracted a purple wallet from it, and from that a snapshot. She handed it to him.

Avoiding a parked car, he glanced at the snapshot, noticing some long stringy blond hair, half-closed eyes, crooked teeth—heavy metal all the way. What a beast.

"You have there a fine-looking dude," Biff said, handing it back.

"That's my Richie!" she said, gazing at the picture. And then—no. He couldn't believe it. Biff simply couldn't believe his eyes: she kissed the picture. He had heard about girls doing this, kissing pictures, but it was one of those things you hear about but never thought happened in real life.

"By the way," she said, "I looked it up in the dictionary."

"Looked what up."

"The verb *peach*. I looked it up while I was getting my coat. I most certainly did not use it correctly. It means—"

"I know what it means," Biff said. "I knew back then. But you two were so busy talking that I couldn't . . ."

"Relax! Okay, I believe you! I looked up *biff* too," she added.

"What?"

"Biff. It's this." She reached out and biffed him on the ear, sharply enough to irritate him. "A light blow or cuff. Something I've had my share of." She laughed softly in a way he hadn't heard from her until now. It was rather pleasant. "I wonder why they named you that? It must have been a real biff to your mother when she found out she was pregnant with you. Or she biffed herself. Or your father." (He refused to smile.) "Actually," she said, "I have a terrible confession, would you like to hear it? I lied. Richie isn't really my boyfriend. He doesn't even know I exist. I just have this giant crush on him. Like whenever I see him? I can't take it, I gelatinize."

Biff kept his eyes straight ahead. *Gelatinize*. Good grief.

"That ever happen to you?" she asked.

"What, gelatinization?"

"No, a crush."

Biff cleared his throat and adjusted the rear-view mirror.

"It *has* happened to you," she said quietly. "My goodness, you're blushing. Tell me."

"Does it really matter?"

"Yes."

"Why?"

"Tell me, Biff, I want to know. I'm interested. It has or *is* happening to you. Isn't it?"

He hesitated. "Kind of."

His face burned. Why had he said that? He felt like he'd just shown her a page of his diary.

"You do know what I'm talking about, then," she said. "You do have a crush on someone?"

"Kind of, I said."

"You don't carry a picture of her, though, do you? No. But you carry her around in your heart. You do, then? Right now?"

"Kind of."

He had never revealed this to anyone. Nobody. Not even Willa. And here he was, suddenly admitting it to this . . . this babe, an hour after meeting her.

"What's her name?" she asked.

He hesitated, then shook his head. No. That was going too far.

"Come on," she said. "I told you Richie's. Tell me. Please?"

"Helen," he lied.

"Helen," she repeated. "Helen . . . Helen what?"

"What difference does it make? You didn't tell me *his* last name."

"Fitzpatrick."

"I don't care."

"Why are you getting so huffy?" she said. "You really *are* gone on old Helen, aren't you. My goodness, the windows are steaming up. This is classic."

Biff's eyes smarted. Heidi finished her cigarette and threw it out the window. He watched it in his rear-view mirror, crash and tumble and shed sparks along the street.

"It really is a lovely old name," Heidi said. "*Helen* . . . Is she fair?"

"She has freckles."

"And hair?"

"She has hair, yes."

"What color? Long or short?"

"Long wavy reddish brown." All of this was true.

"Auburn? Auburn hair?"

"Yes, auburn," Biff said.

"Ah. Auburn. I do like that word. Ah-burn. It makes me think of leafy autumn afternoons. Burnished woods. Claret and hunting dogs. Autumn. Another nice word. Ahh-tumn."

Biff rolled his eyes.

But he did, as a matter of fact, associate Tommie Isaac with, among other things, leafy autumn afternoons and . . . burnished woods, whatever those were. He'd have to look that one up.

"I'll bet she's Irish," Heidi said.

"I don't know."

"What's her last name."

"Not Irish. Look, I'll drop you off somewhere, anywhere you want to go, but I need to go home. I—I have to go home."

"Big Friday night?"

"Yeah, real big."

"I'll bet." She laughed with that soft, breathy laugh.

"Look," he said. "We both know you're not going to the library. I don't even think any are open past six on Friday night. I don't—I don't care where you're going, I'll be glad to drop you off wherever, and I'll be your alibi, if that's what you want. But otherwise—"

"What do you call *this*? Hm?" She unzipped her black bag, revealing several hot-pink and magenta and turquoise paperbacks, the kind with pictures of "cute" girls on the covers. "Does this look like something I'd be taking to meet my drug lord? And I hate to inform you, but the Ballard branch is open till *nine* on Fridays."

"Ballard?" He looked at her; she nodded. "Hooray," he said. "The destination has been revealed."

He hung a U-turn and headed back toward Ballard.

"God," she said, "don't you even know which libraries are open till nine on Friday night in your own hometown? Goodness me, I know all the hours of all the libraries in Spokane. I *love* libraries. Especially on Friday nights, when everyone else is out *par*-dying. I read constantly."

"Gee whiz."

"I've only been here since Wednesday, and I've read all these books."

"Looks like some pretty heavy stuff there," he said. "Sweet Valley High?"

"No." She hadn't realized he was joking. "This one's a series called Cheerleader Pageantry. I've read nineteen out of the twenty-two so far. And there's this other series called Sorority Triplets. About these identical triplets who live in Gamma Gamma Delta . . ."

Just as he had suspected. The mind of a nine-year-old.

"I suppose you think I'm really dumb and shallow for liking those books," she said.

"Heavens no."

"I do admit, I mainly read to escape. I suppose you only read deep, intellectual stuff."

"Well, you know what F.D.R. said: 'A mind is a terrible thing to waste.' "

"You *are* an irritant."

She took out another cigarette and pushed in the lighter.

"Oh, good," Biff said, "I was hoping you'd light up another one."

"What is your problem?" she asked, looking at him.

A few drops of rain spat against the windshield.

"Can I drive for a while?" she asked. "I have my learner's permit, but I never get to practice. The truth is, you see, I do need a little extra practice. Although I'm getting better. I'm really not that bad. Despite what *some* people might try to tell you."

"I don't think I have the right kind of insurance," Biff said.

"Cheapskate."

They drove along in silence. It began to rain harder. Biff turned his wipers on.

"Okay," she said, "what would you recommend? In the way of reading material."

"Oh, Sorority Triplets is hard to top."

"Go ahead, recommend something. I'll read it tonight."

He hesitated. "Reach down there under the seat."

Holding her cigarette in the air with one hand, she felt around under the seat and came up with three paperback books.

"Take your pick," he said. "Or take all three."

He had bought these for a quarter each at a garage sale he'd gone to a few weeks ago. People at garage sales were either extremely nice or extremely sour and greedy or extremely something else, but never the same. If they were nice, he usually tried to buy something from them, more often than not a book.

She held the books up and read their titles aloud.

"*Ulysses* by Homer. Oh, I know how that ends. *The Great Gatsby*. Saw the first half of the amazingly boring movie. *Anthology of Modern Poetry*. Never heard of it, but an intriguing title."

Holding up *Gatsby* again, she asked, "This any good? I like the author's last name—it starts with 'Fitz.' Same as my Richie's."

"Wow."

"It's a short book. I'll read it tonight."

Smoking her cigarette, she turned to page one and began reading.

"You still want to go to the library?" he asked.

"What? No. This'll do. Just take me home, driver. I really only wanted to get out and smoke a couple of ciggies."

"I knew it," he muttered.

She was still reading when he drove past the security guard in the booth and dropped her off at the front door.

"Oh, Biff, would you do me a favor? Return these books for me? They're not due for weeks, but I hate leaving them lying around. I might be leaving very suddenly."

She tossed the paperbacks on the seat where she'd been sitting.

"Thanks for the smokes," she said. "I'll pay you back tomorrow. When you come to dinner, right? Bye, Biff."

Through the raindrops on the passenger window, he watched her open the lobby door. He watched as she waited for the elevator. Even after she had gotten on the elevator and the silver doors had closed, he sat in his car looking out at the rainy night.

CHAPTER SIX

He drove straight to the library, which had indeed closed at six, and shoved her books through the return slot, hoping no one would come along and see what kind of reading material he had, and then drove home slowly along the back streets, thinking about the girl whose books he had just returned, the girl who had snapped and unsnapped her pants in front of him.

It had been a long day; he wasn't used to this much excitement. Tailing his loved one, talking to Pam, meeting a new person—it was all very draining. One of the worst things about meeting a new person was the struggle to make conversation, but not with this girl, holy cow, he'd not had to struggle with her, his tongue hadn't flapped like that since he didn't know when. Yet he couldn't remember much of what they'd said.

She wasn't so bad, he had to admit. It was a nice

change, having another human being in the car besides Ray Hu, cigarette smoke notwithstanding. Why had she said she might be leaving suddenly? Why had she looked up his name in the dictionary? Good lord, why had he told her about Tommie? Well, it probably couldn't do much harm. It was nagging him, though, and he wondered if it was bad luck to have betrayed his secret about Tommie. To that girl, of all people. Well, why not her? At least she seemed more or less in the same boat.

He felt a sudden stab of desire for Tommie. He was definitely running out of time with her. Just a few months—spring and summer—before she headed north to college in the fall. Thank God she wasn't going far, only to Bellingham, an hour and a half drive; he was going to the community college just down the street from Willa's house and he could visit Tommie on weekends. Their relationship could survive that distance, so long as it was on a firm enough foundation.

What was he talking about? *What* relationship?

Another big Friday night. He never did anything. Sometimes he and Ray Hu went out for hamburgers and ate them while driving around listening to the radio and arguing about baseball and life. Or they might end up at the Earl of Nottingham Lanes for some pinball and bowling. Then maybe go get some ice cream or a chocolate-chip cookie or a cinnamon roll. When Ray wasn't with him, Biff would drive by Tommie Isaac's house, or, if she happened to be working that night, he'd hang around outside the Safeway and watch her bag groceries, peering through the store window, quick to scurry around the corner if she came out with someone's groceries. Once in a while he got up the nerve to go inside the store and buy some item. If Tommie saw him—and there was no guarantee she would; she was often too busy—she'd look up, a few strands of hair sticking to her slightly sweaty forehead, the gold chain she sometimes wore catching a gleam of light, and say "Hi!"

He was almost tempted to drive by the supermarket right now to see if she was there, but he decided to go home and eat some dinner and relax and figure out where he'd go for tomorrow's hike. Maybe Paul, Willa's boyfriend, would know of a good secret hike somewhere.

When Biff got home, Willa and Paul happened to be on their way out to dinner and a movie, and, as they often did, they invited Biff to join them, but he declined. Paul said he'd think about a place and let Biff know when they came back from the movie. This was fine with Biff; it gave him some hope and kept him from having to think about it himself. When in doubt, let someone else make the decision for you.

Biff and Willa lived in a huge house on a wooded lot, not far from their old house, the one they'd grown up in. She'd had the house custom-built two years ago, around the time their parents had moved to a place called Pointe Pastorale, in Tempe, Arizona, one of those retirement villages where no one under sixty was allowed. Their father, Wallace Schmurr, Sr., was a fat man with a goatee, who bowled and played the ukulele and wore a set of mechanical pencils in his front shirt pocket. For thirty-five years he had been an algebra and trig teacher at a private secular high school in Seattle, until two years ago, when he was forced to retire at sixty because of his weak heart. Their mother, a frail, nervous woman, was a basket case. She had never recovered from Wallace Jr.'s death ten years ago.

Wallace Jr. would have been twenty-eight if he had

lived. He was killed while driving home from a high-school golf meet in a distant town. He and three other guys on the golf team had all been drinking, and Wallace, who was driving, had pulled over to the side of the road and gotten out of the car to take a leak, and had walked right into an oncoming logging truck.

Sixteen-year-old Willa took charge of the house and family from that point on.

It had been good news, actually, when their mom and dad had agreed to move down south. Willa had talked them into it, and she sent them a check every month; otherwise, they wouldn't have been able to afford a place like Pointe Pastorale. Biff was glad for them. He'd always felt guilty for coming along unexpectedly, when his mom was forty-three and his dad forty-four. They probably *had* biffed themselves when they found out about him.

He prayed they were happy now, maybe happy for the first time in their lives, even his mom, in her own way, if that was possible. God bless those two.

So he had lived with his sister these two years, was supported by her and dependent on her.

Willa was rich. She had gone to college, while still living at home and taking care of the family, but had never graduated or even declared a major because she'd been too busy working as a waitress and making money. She had made a ton of money in tips, because she was such a natural-born people person, invested it in some Pepsi machines, and found places to install them that were so perfect that she made a huge profit, with which she bought a hunk of land, just before the real-estate boom, and had it subdivided and . . . Oh, it was all very complicated, but the bottom line was that she was twenty-six years old and rolling in money. She insisted she was happy, but Biff had his doubts. Sometimes he really worried about his sister.

He went into the kitchen and put some macaroni and cheese into the microwave, and while he was waiting for it to heat up, he went to his dictionary and looked up the word *burnish*. Then he flipped back a few pages to *biff*; then, just out of curiosity, he went to the H's and checked if there was any such word as *heidi*. There wasn't, of course, but she'd have fit nicely between *Heidelberg* and *heifer*.

The microwave dinged; he slid his macaroni and cheese out, squirted catsup over it, and took it to the kitchen table. Using the beagle-dog napkin holder, he propped up his biography of Bob Dylan and read while he ate.

Later, Biff went out for a walk in the rain. The first Friday night of April, nothing to do, nowhere to go. He thought of Tommie Isaac. One of these days, she'd show up at school in her shorts and blue-and-white-striped-knee socks. Biff didn't think he'd be able to handle it.

At midnight, he was back in the kitchen for his nightly ritual of newspaper and two bowls of cereal. He cherished this time. Sometimes during the day he would dream about what two brands of cereal he'd have that night. He usually had ten different brands on hand to choose from. Willa had given him a special shelf for his "cereal library." He would spread the newspaper out on the table, his cereal bowl in front of him, the milk and sugar on his left, that night's two cereal boxes on his right, and he'd read every word of the newspaper, front to back. It took him about an hour. He skipped nothing, but

skimmed over a few things like the classifieds and rec-
ipes. All while shoveling cereal into his mouth.

He had just finished the first two sections and his first
bowl of cereal, when Willa and Paul came home from
the movie. It was clear they'd had, or were having, an
argument. Willa went straight to the dishwasher and began noisily unloading it while Paul yanked open one
drawer after another in search of the ice-cream scoop.
Poor Paul. Biff had always liked him, but felt sorry for
him for being hopelessly hooked on someone like Willa.
He worked in the produce section of a nearby supermarket (not Tommie's) and had known Willa since high
school. They'd been engaged to be married three times
and all three times Willa had backed out.

Biff asked Paul if he had come up with any suggestions
for the hike.

"Oh, yeah, let's see," Paul said, closing his eyes and
looking up at the ceiling. "Um, there's a nice trail that
goes up to Wallace Falls. Might be a *little* crowded on a
Saturday, depending on the weather. And of course Mt.
Si is always pretty this time of year."

Biff shoved a spoonful of Cap'n Crunch into his mouth
and went back to his newspaper. Paul, probably wondering why he hadn't received a thank-you, shrugged
and continued looking for the ice-cream scoop.

The phone rang; Willa answered it.

"He sure is! He's right here!"

Looking up from his newspaper, Biff saw that his sister
was holding the phone out to him with the same big wide
eyes and uppercased O mouth that she used when talking
to babies. She was mouthing words that Biff couldn't
quite read.

Issagrr? A girl? It's a girl?

For the past two years, every time the phone rang, he had thought of Tommie Isaac, if only for a second. Maybe by some miracle . . .

He went over and took the phone from Willa.

"Hello."

"Back already from your big Friday night?"

No miracle. Just the chomping of bubble gum.

"Oh. Hi."

Willa, staring at him, broke into an excited grin. He turned his back on her.

"Well, I finished it," Heidi said.

"Finished what?"

"Gatsby."

"Oh. Fast reader. What did you, uh . . . ?"

His grip around the phone tightened as he could feel his sister's eyes on his back.

"What did I think? Well, I don't know. What did I think . . . I didn't *think* anything. I just felt excited. And very sort of . . . oh, serene, I suppose. Like usually when I finish a book, I just go grab another. But with this book I was very excited. I don't often get like that. I'm not quite as stirred up now, though. I've come down a notch. I'm just hungry. You in bed?"

"Kitchen." He glanced over his shoulder at Willa, who was beaming at him.

"Did you return those books for me?" Heidi asked.

"Yeah," he said. "The library closed at six."

"Did it. You going to bed?"

"Eventually."

"Would you like some breakfast?"

"What?"

"Would you like to come over and take me out for breakfast."

"Now?"

He heard his sister giggle over his shoulder. Feeling his face turn red, he bent over and leaned on the counter, changing ears with the phone.

Heidi was saying, "I know this place that's open all night and it has these huge omelets and they give you a big plate of the best hash browns. And when you're finished you sit there and have a bottomless cup of coffee. It's not far from here."

"Isn't there, uh . . ."

"What? Speak up."

"A curfew or something . . . for people your age?"

"Oh, Biff, you are completely weird," she said. "Want to?"

"Uh . . ."

"Oh, come on. I'll wait for you out front."

Biff stood there holding the phone after she had hung up. He turned around and faced his sister.

In a hushed voice Willa said, "Paul, look at Biffy. He looks dazed."

" 'Bewitched, Bothered, and Bewildered,' " Paul said, chuckling.

Biff hung up the phone gently and cleared his throat. "Willa, could I borrow a few bucks?"

"Who is she, Bippy?" his sister asked, reaching for her purse.

"Pam's niece," he said. "What do you know about her, anyway?"

"Pam's niece? Which one? She's got three—Happy, Coco, Heidi. Happy and Coco belong to Gary. They're both under ten and weird. You must mean Heidi. . . .

Let's see, isn't she the juvenile delinquent? Paul, Biffy has a date with a juvenile delinquent, isn't it exciting? You're going out right now? A midnight rendezvous! Bippy, you'd better get some gas. Did you know you left your window rolled down? Your car smells like cigarettes."

Biff smoothed out the bills she had handed him and put them in his wallet, not quite sure what was happening. Was this a date? A midnight rendezvous? He was not used to things moving so fast. Yes, dazed was the right word. He'd been dazed all evening. Dazed for most of his life. He only knew that instead of having his second bowl of cereal and then crawling into bed at the usual hour, he was going on the first date of his life, sort of.

The phone rang again. Oh, good. Heidi was probably calling to cancel. Or to say it was all a big joke. Willa answered it again.

"Hi, Pam!"

Pam had probably found out and was nixing the whole thing. Even so, Biff went downstairs and put on a fresh shirt. He tried to comb his hair but it was like trying to comb a shrub. Well, at least he had his pleasant odor. It came from all the showers he took, using a secret brand of soap that had the same fragrance as a Christmas tree and could only be bought at a particular gift shop in the Pike Place Market. "Doesn't my little brother smell like Christmas?" Willa often commented to her friends. "Go ahead, smell him, he doesn't mind."

When Biff came back up to the kitchen, he asked Willa what Pam had wanted.

"Oh, she was just checking up, that's all. She thought maybe Heidi was giving her a story. If it were anyone but you coming to pick up her niece, Bippy, she'd put her foot down and say absolutely not, no way, she'd lock her in. I think there *is* a curfew in this city for people under sixteen. Biffy, don't tell Heidi her aunt doesn't trust her.''

Biff nodded. There was something pathetic about being the kind of guy an aunt would trust her fifteen-year-old niece with at one in the morning.

CHAPTER SEVEN

It was 12:42 a.m. and raining lightly when Biff left the house. Traffic was sparse. He stopped for gas and then pulled over to the coin-operated vacuum cleaner and began cleaning out his car.

He knew he was stalling and he wondered if he shouldn't just call this thing off; phone Heidi and tell her his car wouldn't start or his tooth had abscessed or something. He dreaded these pressure situations. It was his theory that an accumulation of them shortened your life. How nice it would be to go back to the kitchen and have his second bowl of cereal and not shorten his life.

Oh, relax, he told himself. Why can't you just take these things in stride? How about a little humor and merriment? He ran his fingers through his hair. Maybe he should have taken a shower to dampen his hair, make this mess of weeds sit down. But what was he getting so hyped up about? It wasn't really a *date*. Just a girl wanting breakfast. Probably expected him to pay for it, too. Or she had some friend she was going to meet, some fellow juvenile delinquent, and she needed Biff as her alibi. But why fret and stew over all this? Why not make the best of it? Look at it as practice for Tommie.

He got down on the floor in the back seat, dragging the big vacuum-cleaner hose with him and tugging on one of the seat belts, which had gotten wedged down inside the seat. He stuck his hand down there to pull the buckle free, half expecting something to bite him, and his fingertips came in contact with the smooth cover of a paperback book. Pulling it out, he looked at the cover and grinned: *47 Secret Hikes in the Olympic Mountains.*

"I'm picking someone up out front," he told the guard at the front gate.

"A date?" the guard said.

"No, not a date."

"Who would you be dating this time of night, young fella?"

"Here she comes, I see her coming," Biff said. Heidi had spotted him and was walking out to the car.

"Little young to be going out on a date this time of night, ain't you, miss?" the guard said. "Your aunt and uncle know about this?"

Heidi breezed by him.

Biff thought about getting out of the car to open the door for her—would someone like Tommie expect it?— but he was too late; Heidi was already getting in.

Loosen up, he coached himself. Think "humor and merriment."

"Your aunt and uncle know about this, miss?" Biff said.

"Hey, got any more of that bubble gum? Accept any rides from any three-legged camels lately?"

She gave him a look as she lit her cigarette.

"Ah, I see you've found matches," he said. "Could you, uh, crack your window open a little?"

She rolled her eyes. So much for humor and merriment. He shifted into drive and took off, figuring she'd tell him where to go, and he reached out and turned on the radio and pressed his favorite button, continuous seek, which stopped at each station for five seconds and then went on to the next.

"You cleaned out your car," she said.

"Yeah, I found this book I'd been—oh, never mind. Uh, where're we going, by the way? Where is this place?"

"Could you try to calm down? You're making me nervous."

Once again Biff found himself in the ridiculous position of driving without a destination. Drumming his fingers on the steering wheel, he thought, I suppose we're not even going out for breakfast. She just wants a chauffeur.

"I'm a little this side of hungry," he said, admiring his use of colorful language. "How about yourself?"

No reply.

"Is this a good place we're, uh . . . ?"

She finally broke out with a laugh and looked at him, her eyes shining. "Biff, you are—has anyone ever told you you are really weird?"

"Well," he said, "as a matter of fact . . ."

"It's on the west side of Aurora Avenue, directly across the street from Greenlake. Happy now?" she asked.

"Oh," he said. "Grig's or Gig's or something?"

"Grig's."

Oh, God, no. Of all places. Whenever he happened to drive by that joint, he always wondered how a sleazy dive like that could stay in business.

"How, uh . . . how do you know Grig's?" he asked her. "I mean, living in Spokane."

"My father and I go there."

Biff's ears perked up. "Marc Hamilton?"

She nodded. "I visit him every six weeks or so. I take the late train and it gets in around one in the morning, and he picks me up at the station and we go to Grig's and have breakfast and talk and have coffee and wait around and then catch the early ferry over to the islands, which is where he lives, on one of the islands. He has a very large estate."

"Why didn't he pick you up this time?" Biff asked. "How come you're staying with Pam and Lynn?"

"Because," Heidi said, after a moment's hesitation, "I haven't decided whether I'm going to see him this time."

"Why not?"

"Personal reasons."

"Oh."

"When I turn sixteen," she said, "I'm going to buy a car."

"Ah," he said, nodding.

"And then I won't take the train anymore and we probably won't go to Grig's anymore. It'll be the end of something. But I'm actually thinking about moving in with him. My father."

"No kidding?" Biff said.

"He'd like me to. He wants me to move in with him and take care of him and his house, but I haven't made up my mind yet."

Biff nodded, wanting to hear more about her father but not able to think of anything to ask her. "You really might move here? What would you do about school? Transfer or something?"

"I have no idea. I go there with other people, too."

"Where? School?"

"No, Grig's."

"Oh."

"I know people in this area. I have this friend Matt who belongs to the Seattle Tennis Club. I don't like him. He's short and rich and wears a long coat with a fur collar. I have this other friend who I like a lot, she lives up in Everett. Rochelle. She dropped out of high school and got her GED, and now she goes to beauty school."

"Huh," Biff said. To himself he said, I told you so. What'll you bet old Matt or Rochelle or one of her other "friends" is going to come waltzing into Grig's.

"I'm saving up for one," she said.

"You lost me."

"A car," she said.

"Oh."

"I can't wait till I get my license. I know exactly what kind of car I'm going to get, the make, model, color, everything. Do you have to have such a grouchy look on your face?"

"I wasn't aware I . . ."

"You must be thinking unclean thoughts. Are you thinking unclean thoughts? I don't have any bubble gum, if that's what's bothering you."

"Maybe you could aim your smoke a little more toward the window."

She laughed. "Are you this weird all the time?"

Heading north along Aurora Avenue, he was tempted

to swerve off the road and drive the car into Greenlake. That would shake her up. But the sooner they got to Grig's, the sooner this "outing" would be over. If only it were Tommie sitting there.

"I can't picture you playing tennis," she said.

"I can't imagine why you'd bring that up at this moment."

"Grouch! Is it so far past your beddy-bye time?"

Don't let her push your buttons, he told himself.

"Actually, I can't picture you doing a lot of things," she said. "About the only thing I can picture you doing is maybe running around a big field in Bermuda shorts with a net, catching butterflies. Or lawn bowling with old men. Wearing those baggy white slacks and a wide-brimmed straw hat." She laughed suddenly and tossed her head back on the seat. "Maybe it's past *my* bedtime!"

"For the record, I do bowl," he said, blushing and not looking at her. "Regular bowling, not lawn bowling."

"I know," she said.

He glanced at her. "You do?"

"Pam told me. I bowl too, by the way. I'd kill you."

He shook his head. "Oh, no. No, I guarantee you wouldn't."

"You don't know me," she said. "I am very competitive."

"Pam told you I bowl?"

"M-hm. She told me your life story. The only thing she didn't—or couldn't—tell me about was Helen."

"Who?"

"*Helen*, silly. The girl of your dreams?"

Biff swung his face around. "For some reason, I had the idea that was confidential."

"I didn't *tell* Pam anything. I just asked her if she knew

of anybody named Helen who you might be interested in."

"I don't believe it!" He was shaking his head, gripping the wheel with both hands. "If I'd known you were going to go squawking to Pam . . ."

"I didn't *squawk.*"

"I'm just glad I didn't tell you her *real* name!"

"Oh, you gave me a fake, did you? I don't think I believe you. You wouldn't be so touchy if *Helen* wasn't her real name. Why, I simply mention the word *Helen* and I can see your heart flutter. On the other hand, maybe that explains why Pam didn't have the slightest—oh, good, here we are."

Here they were, all right. The dump called Grig's. As he pulled over, his front tire scraped the curb. They sat in the car looking out at the place. A true dump.

Heidi turned and faced him. "I guess I didn't have any right to tell Pam. I'm sorry. I didn't tell her *much.* You're not mad, are you?"

Biff shrugged. "Can I ask you a question? Just out of curiosity?"

"I suppose."

"It's kind of bothering me."

"Go ahead," she said. "And no, I'm not Portuguese."

"What kind of car is it you want?"

"Ah." She smiled. Her lips stretched smooth and pink across her face. It was a nice face, Biff had to admit. The teeth were maybe a little too big, but the rest of the features were pretty much flawless. Pretty and flawless.

"A white Plymouth Reliant," she said, tossing her cigarette out the window. "When I turn sixteen, I'll go out looking for one, and when I find it, I'll buy it."

"A white Plymouth Reliant."

"M-hm."

"Why a white Plymouth Reliant?"

"Because," she said, "I like the name. It's *reliant*. Plus, it looks like an unmarked police car."

Biff nodded, giving her a furtive glance. "Uh, yeah."

"Think I can find a used one for under ten thousand?"

"Dollars? Heidi, I'd shoot for half that."

"Well good. We going in or not?"

They got out of the car. Heidi's cigarette sat burning on the sidewalk. Biff squashed it, picked it up, and tossed it in a trash can.

"You are so weird," she said, laughing.

"Why, because I don't like cigarette butts strewn all over my city?"

"So weird!"

CHAPTER EIGHT

They sat across from each other in a booth with torn upholstery, crumbs, and dried catsup. The linoleum table had just been wiped off and Biff could see the wet streaks and smell the dishrag. They took off their coats. A waitress came with coffee and sticky menus. The coffee cups were white and ceramic and heavy. The coffee tasted good. Heidi ordered a cheese omelet; Biff, a short stack.

"And hash browns," he added.

"They all come with hash browns, honey," the waitress told him.

"But enough hash browns, that's the thing," Biff said.

"Honey," the waitress said, "we'll give you so many hash browns you won't know what to do." She walked away.

Biff looked around the place. His eyes lit on an old pinball machine in the far corner. His two flipper-fingers twitched. Slowly his right hand slipped inside his pocket but ran into a Teeny Bouncer before finding a quarter. He pulled the Teeny Bouncer out and dribbled it on the table while eyeing the machine. Pretty soon, he was able to look away. He noticed a line of dead flies along the windowsill. Up at the counter, two unshaved men sat slumped on red stools, drinking coffee. There was no one else in the place. He looked back at the pinball machine and wiped his palms on his thighs.

He looked at Heidi.

"I'm curious," he said.

She was lighting a cigarette. She dropped the smoldering match into the glass ashtray where a dead fly sat. She leaned forward, smiling, blowing out smoke. "Yes?"

"Why do you care if it looks like an unmarked police car?"

"Because," she said, "then other drivers will never *really* be sure I'm not a cop."

"Oh . . ."

"People drive like maniacs," she added, gazing out the window.

He remembered that her mother had been killed in a car accident. Maybe that had something to do with what she was talking about, although he couldn't imagine what. He considered telling her that Wallace Jr. had died in a car accident, too. But he decided not to pursue it.

He looked at her hands, her numerous silver rings and bracelets. A chunk of ash was forming on the end of her cigarette.

"Why did you get suspended?" he asked.

"Oh, let's not go into that right now. I want to ask you something." She met his eyes. "I want to ask you, do you ever wonder what life would be like if you *had* her?"

"Had who?"

"Helen, of course."

"What do you mean, had her."

"You know, belonged to each other, loved each other. Don't you wonder if meeting the right person and being in love with that person could really—could really change your life? I mean *change* it? Like sometimes I think, if only I had Richie Fitzpatrick, then suddenly everything would be *bearable*—or more than just bearable. School and home and friends would all seem . . . good. But of course they wouldn't really be different; nothing would have changed, really, except *I'd* be different. Does that make any sense? Do you feel that way sometimes? With Helen? If that's her real name. Is it her real name?"

For a second, Biff lost himself in her eyes. He tried to remember what she'd said about *The Great Gatsby*, something about being stirred up.

"Biff, is Helen her real name?"

He shook his head.

"Tell me her real name. But first"—she leaned even closer to him across the table—"first, I'm going to guess. Because I have this hunch. I'm going to guess that it's Pam."

"Pam what?"

"Pam you're secretly in love with."

Biff stared. "Pam Kobleska?"

She nodded.

"Pam *Kobleska*?" he said again.

She nodded again.

Slowly, a smile came to Biff's face. "Pam Kobleska. Now that's funny."

He began to laugh. He wasn't quite sure why—why is anything funny? It wasn't so much the idea of Pam Kobleska being the girl of his dreams; it was Heidi's *seriousness* about it. That's what got him.

He laughed in quick tommy-gun bursts and then went into his rare silent crackup. Tears spilled down his cheeks. He put his face flat on the table and wept with laughter.

The waitress came over and refilled their coffee cups. Biff lifted his head. The waitress gave the table a wipe where his face had been.

"Perhaps you think I'm drunk," he said to the waitress, wiping his eyes.

"Honey, I know a drunk when I see one." She walked away.

"Honey, that's the first time I've seen you laugh," Heidi said, smiling at him and patting the table with her hands and making her silver bracelets clack.

"Honey, it felt good," he said. "And no, I assure you, it's not Pam."

"Then tell me her name."

He took a deep breath, held it, and finally let go. "Tommie. Tomassa Isaac. Tommie." He closed his eyes. When he opened them, he was still there. No bolt of lightning.

He had no idea why, but he started to talk about her. And once he started he couldn't stop. He told about the first time he saw Tommie. He told about Tommie's job at the supermarket. About the incident in the hall last Friday. About driving by her house 184 times. He told about the time he'd followed Tommie to the dentist's office; the time he'd driven by her house and seen her and her father trying to load a desk into her father's car and how he'd been tempted to get out and offer them a hand; he told about the time he was watching her play volleyball and she'd said "damn" when she served it out of bounds; the time she'd dropped her books in the library and her face turned bright red.

He caught his breath when the waitress brought their orders. Both came with a mountain of hash browns. They took turns pouring the catsup. The hash browns were crispy brown on the outside. His pancakes were thin, the way they should be, not thick and doughy. He surveyed the choices of syrup: maple, blueberry, boysenberry . . . What was this white stuff? Coconut. Hmm. Now, that was intriguing. Normally he didn't like experimenting with unknown food, especially at 1:30 in the morning, but he poured the white coconut syrup over his butter-melted pancakes and took a bite.

"How are they?" Heidi asked.

"The fourth best I've had in my life."

She laughed and shook her head. "All right, continue," she said. "More about Tommie. More more more."

So he told her. He told her everything. He'd kept Tommie Isaac inside him for two years, and now that he was finally sharing her, she seemed more real, less of a dream. Not that it wasn't pretty embarrassing, opening his heart like this. But to hear her name out loud in his own voice, rather than echoing around the caverns of his mind, was exhilarating. Heidi kept pumping him for details, laughing softly now and then. Surprisingly, rather than inhibiting him, her laughter made Biff light-headed and giddy.

The waitress took away their empty plates and came back with more coffee.

"You kids get enough to eat?"

"The fourth most stuffed I've ever been in my life," Heidi said, smiling at Biff. She ordered a bowl of vanilla ice cream with a small amount of chocolate sauce, and when the waitress brought it to her she spooned some of her coffee onto it.

"You leave for Spokane next Friday?" Biff asked her.

"Unless I decide to accept my father's offer. He's asked me to—I told you, didn't I?"

"To live with him, yes," Biff said, nodding. "But you said you might not even see him. For personal reasons. You might live with him or you might not even see him. That's puzzling."

"Isn't it," she said. "By the way, don't say anything to Pam about it—my father's offer."

"Why not?"

"Because she'll tell Gran and Gary and Sherri. They don't even like me visiting my father. If they knew I was thinking about living with him, they'd . . ."

"They'd what?"

"Make life unpleasant."

"But I don't see—"

"Biff, it's all very complicated. Just don't mention it to Pam, okay?"

He shrugged. "Okay."

She ladled more spoonfuls of coffee onto her ice cream. Then she pushed the bowl toward him. "Why don't you have this. I have to make a phone call."

Biff watched her walk to the pay phone by the rest rooms. She dialed a zero, which meant she was calling long distance. Calling who? Gary and Sherri in Spokane? Her father across the Sound? Or maybe that beauty-school babe up in Everett.

He glanced at his watch: 2:41. He could be in bed a little after three, sleep a few hours, then look through the *Secret Hikes* book for the ideal place to—

A man had just come in and sat down in the next booth, facing Biff. The man had only a left arm; the right one was an empty sleeve that had been sewn up. He was slop-faced drunk. The waitress brought him some coffee. He shook his head no to a menu. He looked unsteadily around the room and his eyes landed on Biff. It seemed to take him a moment to bring Biff's face into focus. Biff looked away.

"Pardon me, miss. I wonder if I might be so bold as to trouble you for a cigarette."

Biff tapped a Now out of Heidi's pack and handed it to the one-armed man, who had to come around the table to get it.

"May I further trouble you for a light, since I am a bit shorthanded."

Biff struck a match on the third try and held it to the tip of the man's cigarette. The man sucked deeply.

"Most grateful, miss."

Biff felt pleased. There is comradeship between a man who gives another man a cigarette, even if one man thinks the other's a Miss.

The waitress brought the check and put it face down on the table. Biff looked over at Heidi's melting ice cream and then at Heidi, who had just hung up the phone and gone into the rest room. Short phone call, he thought. Just long enough to say, "Break out the booze and bongs, Rochelle, we're on our way." He turned the check over, used his father's method to compute the tip at fifteen percent, left the tip on the table, and went to the cash register.

The one-armed man was telling the waitress that he wanted a salad. "The *heart* of the salad. *Heart* of the salad, you hear? If it's not the *heart* of the salad, I don't wannit, you taggit outa my vishinity . . ."

Biff left the exact change for the check on top of the glass counter and went over to the pinball machine, fingering a quarter that was in his pocket.

He studied the machine. It was an oldie. Ancient. From the Long Ago. Pre-video games. It was called Ski Bum. It showed a picture of studly fellows and buxom girls flirting on the ski slopes. He'd never played this machine but it looked basic enough: simply knock down two banks of flags, twice, and then go for the "Specials" when they lit up. Piece of cake. Hard to pass up. One quick game wouldn't hurt, would it? No harm in one game. At least it wasn't Buildup . . .

His hand trembled as he inserted the quarter.

Ahhh. The musical tinkle of the quarter falling through the mechanism. The machine clicked itself back to zero and came to life.

The first silver ball plopped into position. Biff pulled back the lever and launched the ball into play, getting the feel of the machine as the ball pinged and ponged between bumpers. It had a slight lean to the left; these old machines usually did lean one way or the other. And slow motion, compared to the modern ones; these oldies were meant to be played with patience and precision, not the flailing high-tech whirligig gimmickry of the modern machines. Take your shots wisely. Aim. One flag at a time. Trap the ball with the flippers. Control. Choose your target.

Heidi came out of the rest room and watched him for a minute. She didn't ask about the check.

"I'm about to win a game," he said.

"Whoopee."

"Not bad for my first quarter in twelve days. Left flipper's a bit sticky, but she's not in bad shape for her age.

Notice, all I have to do is hit that Special when it comes on. Watch. There it is. Now if I can just trap the ball with the left flipper. Like that. Okay. Clutch shot. Here we go. One, two, three, shoot."

He missed. The ball took a bad bounce and he lost it down the left side. He ended up just sixty points from winning a free game. His jaw was sore from grinding his teeth.

"Hey, Heidi, you mind if I—" He turned around. She was gone.

Outside, the light steady rain was still falling. He looked in his car but she wasn't there. His seat was wet because he'd left his window rolled down. His car smelled like cigarettes. He tossed his jacket into the car without opening the door, and looked around.

She was nowhere in sight.

He walked up to the end of the block and stood on the corner. There were no cars. The rain fell softly on his face. He burped coconut syrup.

Finally, he saw her. She was way down by the lake, just standing there, looking out.

He crossed the street, hopping over the center barrier, and came up behind her.

"Sorry," he said. "I got a little carried away with that pinball."

"Why are you sorry? You have a perfect right to play. Go back and play all night if you want."

"What's wrong?"

She didn't answer for a minute. Then she turned to him and spoke in a strange, distant voice.

"What's wrong? I hate it when you spend time with somebody and you think you're getting to know them and you go to the rest room and when you come out they're playing pinball. I hate that. Not being able to trust somebody. I hate it when people aren't *reliant*. Like when you call somebody three times and leave a message on their stupid answering machine and they don't bother to call you back. Listen, Biff, why don't you just call her up."

"Who?"

"Tommie."

"Oh, I . . ."

"If I were Tommie, I'd be glad to go out with you one time."

"You would?"

"Sure. You have to remember, Biff, she's as shy as you are. Maybe more. She'll understand. You don't give her enough credit. Or yourself, either. She did, after all, like your essay. Call her up."

He nodded, looking out across the lake. "Maybe I will."

"Well, good. The sooner the better. You've wasted enough time."

"It's just that you're talking about a major overhaul of my personality," he said glumly.

She laughed and started walking.

Back in the car, Biff drove slowly. They didn't say much.

"I'm, uh, taking you home, correct?" he asked.

She was in mid-yawn. "Where else would you be taking me?"

"Just making sure."

When he got to the condos, he dimmed his headlights and the guard waved them through. He left his car idling and walked with her to the lobby entrance.

"Heidi, I'm sorry about that pinball stuff. It's like a disease with me."

"I told you not to be sorry. You're going to call her tomorrow, right?"

"Tommie? I—well I-I—well I haven't . . ."

"I see," she said, thinking. "Well, I suppose it wouldn't matter if you waited till next week. Are you doing anything tomorrow?—or today or whatever it is. You're coming over for dinner, right? Would you like to do something before that?"

"With you?"

"M-hm."

"Well, I—I've been kind of planning on getting away for a . . . but I . . . Well, yeah, I'd like to."

"I sleep late, but come as early as you want."

"All right . . . I'll do that."

She turned and let the lobby door slam shut. For the third time that day, that long day, Biff watched her vanish behind the silver elevator doors.

CHAPTER NINE

Biff didn't go straight home but drove around in the rain, thinking. His tires sizzled along the empty, slick streets. His window was down to air out the smoke. It was 3:28 Saturday morning. He wasn't sleepy. His occasional burps tasted of coffee, catsup, and coconut syrup. He needed to drive and think.

He thought of that one-armed man, ranting about the heart of the salad. What, precisely, was the heart of the salad? The center of the lettuce? Or something more symbolic? He thought of that moment of comradeship in lighting the man's cigarette: why had he found it so satisfying?

He yawned and drove along slowly. His left sleeve was wet from the window being down. He wouldn't get much sleep tonight, but so what, it was spring vacation.

He yawned again and thought of Heidi. Why had she been so interested in Tommie? Almost hungry for details. He didn't regret blabbing to her about Tommie. He felt excited, stimulated, confused—but not sorry. But when the sun came up? Things you did at night could be pretty embarrassing in the light of day. Of course, things you did in the day could seem downright idiotic at night, too. The safest policy, he believed, was to avoid doing anything you might regret, ever.

What about calling Tommie? Would he ever muster the gumption—the "heart"—to call her? Heidi had laughed when he said it would take a major overhaul of his personality. What was funny about needing a whole new stinking life?

Biff turned up into the hills, automatically heading toward Tommie's house. He wondered what Tommie would be doing next week. Working extra hours at the grocery store, probably. Saving her money for college. Once again, at the thought of fall coming, he felt a stab of panic.

He turned down her street and saw her car parked in front of her house. The house was dark, the porch light off. A cat darted into his headlight beams and shot under a parked car. Cutting it a little close there, cat. That was all he needed, to nail a cat in front of Tommie's house.

He continued up the street to the next block, to the parking lot of Brookdale Elementary. Good old Brookdale. Fourth, fifth, sixth grade—those were the greatest years. He hadn't been a bit shy back then. Far from it. Sneaking up behind Sandra Fenning and yanking down her knee sock. The nerve! The momentary thrill of feeling his hands shimmy down a girl's smooth calf. Holy cow.

The shyness had come in seventh or eighth grade. What had brought it on? Hormones or something. Some boys got zits or hair on their chest; Biff just got antisocial. In eighth grade, the thought of yanking down a girl's knee sock would have stopped his heart.

Here in the parking lot of good old Brookdale, his heart began to ache with self-pity for who he'd become. How pathetic that his most thrilling memory was pulling down a homely girl's knee sock in fifth grade. How depressing that his high-school career was just about over and he'd devoted twenty-three months to . . . to what? Longing for Tommie!

What about next year? There'd be plenty of girls in community college. They'd be swarming. Lots of them better-looking than Tommie. But they were swarming *this* year—why hadn't he ever been struck by any other girl? The sight of Tommie Isaac in those shorts and blue-and-white-striped knee socks, or working at the grocery store, her hair pulled back, her neck slightly sweaty, her sport shirt unbuttoned at the collar, her freckles and baby fat, it was enough to—

Agh. He bit down on the steering wheel. There was no other way to relieve his tormented soul.

He was losing it, all right. He was cracking up.

The thought of Tommie Isaac moved him even more profoundly than the dark afternoons when he stood at his brother Wallace's grave.

He drove home, let himself in, turned off the porch light, and emptied his pockets onto the hall stand—keys, wallet, two Teeny Bouncers. Willa would know where to find his wallet.

Biff slept until almost nine. His alarm went off while

he was in the shower. He finished dressing and went upstairs to have a look in his wallet.

Sure enough, it had sprouted fresh money overnight —a crinkled twenty and two humble ones. A miracle.

He sat down at the kitchen table and had a piece of toast. While he ate, he flipped through one of Willa's self-help books which she happened to have left out. He had a suspicion that she left them lying around on purpose so that he would read them. He skimmed a chapter called "The Three Biggest Steps on the Pathway to Success," and one called "Knock the T Off Can't." Books like this made him ache for Tommie. When he finished his toast, he grabbed his keys and two Teeny Bouncers and scribbled a quick note to Willa, who had gone to her archery lesson.

Willa,
   Thanks for the money. Will pay you back in twelve years. Make that thirteen. Will mail you a check. Am going out with Heidi today and having dinner (later) at Pam and Lynn's.
                    Love,
                    Your Illustrious Brother, Biff

He read the note and crossed out "Heidi" and wrote "The Niece" above it. Then he crossed out "ustrious," which just left "Ill," and put the note in the usual place, under the beagle napkin-holder.

It was a gray, drizzly morning but with the feel of spring in the air. No need for his jacket. He stood in the light seeping rain looking up and down the street at the tall firs. So quiet.

75

Willa's house was at the end of the cul de sac, perched above seven other houses, all of which were only two years old. The lawns were two years old, most of the cars two years old or less, everything was perfect and well taken care of. People weren't allowed to park boats in their driveway, it was against the rules of the agreement that you had to sign in order to live here, the neighborhood "covenants" that said you had to keep your lawn mowed and couldn't paint your house some outlandish color, and your teenage kid couldn't play his trumpet in the driveway or park his old beater there, and you were strongly urged, but not required, to put up Christmas lights but you had to take them down by January 31.

His stomach gurgled. He was still burping coconut syrup.

His hair, damp from his morning shower, became even wetter as he stood in the rain. He gave his head a vigorous dog-shake. The wetter the better. It was when it dried out that it stiffened up like wire, like a spiky wool helmet. When it was dry, if he'd wanted to, he could have walked around with a whole assortment of things inserted in it —pens, pencils, toothbrush, fork and spoon.

His sister Willa's hair was thick, too, but not as curly as his, and a little darker, like their mother's. Willa's face was extremely pale. She would have made a good vampire. Unlike her brother, she wore makeup. She hated her knobby knees. All through junior high and high school she'd been a taunted, shy, pale, skinny runt, and then suddenly she'd blossomed when she hit twenty-two or twenty-three, and started making all that money.

As far as Biff knew, she'd never read a book in her adult life, except for the twenty-some self-help books that she kept on a shelf in her bedroom. They had all been written back in the 1950s and had titles like *You Can Achieve Anything You Desire, Ten Principles for Success, Believing in You, Positive Imaging, Energizing Your Life, Releasing Your Inner Powers*, and so on. Willa and Paul often argued about believing in yourself and positive imaging and that sort of thing. Paul said it was all horse manure. Biff usually left the room during their arguments because he found the whole issue frustrating and paradoxical. He wanted to believe in himself and in his inner powers but he wanted even more to believe in something infinitely greater and beyond himself, something that was all spirit and all powerful and all loving, something that was love itself, something that could cure the world of evil as well as make the phone ring one evening and have it be Tommie Isaac on the other end.

He waited for Heidi in the Kobleskas' living room.

"May be a while," Pam came out to say, still in her robe and slippers. "I just rousted her out of bed and now I'm French-braiding her hair. Lynn's already left for the library. Help yourself to something in the kitchen, Biffy."

"No hurry."

He got up and trudged to the kitchen, muttering "French-braid." Whatever that was. It sounded like a form of torture or kinky sex. He could feel his hair drying out, thickening, hardening up like concrete.

Taking a glass of grape juice with him, he opened the sliding glass door that led out onto the wet and windy balcony, slid the door closed behind him, and stood in the rain, looking out at the Sound. A freighter, piled with rectangular railroad cars, was heading north up the passage, on its way to the Strait of Juan de Fuca, which would take it out to the Pacific. Biff imagined being a deckhand, taking a last look at Seattle, at this harbor, this building with its balconies, this wild-haired kid on the balcony holding a grape juice, and he envied that kid up there for not being a deckhand on a freighter, yet not realizing that that kid had a whole set of pressure situations of his own.

He held his glass out in the rain. Funny, the rain didn't go in, it just hit the sides, his hand, his wrist. The April wind came from the Sound and carried a chill from the Olympics. But he could feel, smell, and taste spring. Moments like this, he ached for Tommie. He didn't know what he'd do if he couldn't have her. Sometimes he felt that he was slipping, going over the edge. Just like his mom. And his dad, too, with his bowling and ukulele. And even Willa, buying things and piling up more crap and making more money and believing in herself and worrying about her biological clock. Face it, his family wasn't too normal, except for Wallace Jr., who was dead.

We all worry about something, he thought. We all want. In that essay on love he'd written and dedicated to Tommie, he had talked about the Twenty-third Psalm, which began "The Lord is my shepherd; I shall not want." What were they talking about, "I shall not want"? How can you not want something? Biff knew exactly what he wanted. "He maketh me to lie down in green pastures: he leadeth me beside the still waters. He restoreth my soul . . ." *That* was love and that was all he wanted. A worthy goal. The only goal.

And just think: Tommie had heard his essay and thought about him while hearing it, and taken the time to come up to him in the hall and—

Next week! By God! He'd call her next week. But he'd

go on that hike first and think about what he was going to say to her.

Biff went back to the living room, just as Heidi came out with her blond hair pulled back and braided intricately. She was wearing a big sweatshirt, rather tight black pants, white socks, and white tennis shoes. Holding her head erect, she seemed quite pleased with the hairdo. Biff noticed her ears, which he hadn't seen before and which were now exposed and naked except for the white loop earrings dangling from them.

"Too bad the weather's such a drag," Pam said. "Biffy, I think you should give Heidi a tour of Seattle. All your favorite haunts. Go somewhere nice for lunch, but make sure you come back hungry for dinner. We'll eat somewhere between eight and ten, how's that sound? Which reminds me, I think we set our clocks ahead tonight. Spring ahead, fall back. We lose an hour. Heidi, don't make Biffy pay for everything. You buy lunch. Have fun, kiddos. Call if you're going to be later than eightish. Take my umbrella. I'm going back to bed."

Heidi wanted coffee, so Biff headed for the Lucky 4 U grocery store where he'd bought the cigarettes yesterday. Why did he want to go back there? As a test. Today he was going to do only Good. The more Good you do, the more likely you are to achieve whatever you desire. He had read that in Willa's self-help book this morning.

This time Heidi came in with him. The same old man in the green apron was sitting behind the counter, reading the newspaper. He glanced up at Biff and showed no recognition. So far, so Good.

Heidi filled a Styrofoam cup with black coffee and

stuck a plastic lid on it. Biff opened the cooler (a grave misnomer) and felt the small plastic containers of orange juice to see if any of them were cold. He hated lukewarm orange juice. He could feel the man staring at him. He's going to test me, Biff thought. He's going to try to push my buttons. Not this time. Remember, this is a test.

"No cancer sticks today, cowboy?" the man said, when Biff put his orange juice on the counter next to Heidi's coffee.

"Nope," Biff said.

Heidi spilled a handful of bubble gum on the counter and looked from Biff to the old man.

"You're sure now," the man said.

Biff felt his pulse quicken. "Yep."

The man grinned and adjusted his glasses. "Say, you're not thinking of putting vodka in that orange juice and making a screwdriver, are you? Guy as mature as you, why, he can probably walk into any liquor store in the State of Washington and not even get carded. Heh-heh. Whassa matter, you shy today, cowpoke?"

The total came to $1.07. Biff opened his wallet, skipped over his two ones, found his twenty, and placed it on the counter.

The man's face sank. His bloated hand picked up the twenty. "You, uh, got anything smaller'n this, cowpoke? I'm a little short on change today. This'll clean out my till."

Biff shook his head. Already he was beginning to feel lousy. In a small but mean-spirited way, he had done injury to this man, and so to the whole human family, himself included. Needless to say, he had just flunked his test.

Biff took the change and left without saying anything. The bell above the door tinkled.

"Meanie," Heidi said outside. It was unclear whether she was referring to the old man or to himself, but Biff knew.

CHAPTER TEN

The tour began with a destination of Heidi's: the house she'd lived in with her mother and father during the second four years of her life (the first four were in an apartment complex which she didn't remember). She directed him to a brown one-story house on a hill overlooking Greenlake to the southwest.

Biff pulled up alongside the curb. "Want to get out?"

"It used to be white," she said quietly, looking out her window. The way her hands were folded in her lap reminded Biff of Sunday school. She gave her head a quick shake and turned to him. "And that is really all I have to say. I refuse to remember anything . . . I refuse. Let's go, driver. Why did I want to come here in the first place? It holds no memory for me."

Her hands unfolded and, the only time he'd ever seen them do something awkwardly, fumbled for a cigarette.

Biff drove away from the curb.

"Show me where you live," she said, after lighting up. "Something much more pleasant, I'm sure. Your sister's house, that's what I want to see. I've heard about it from Pam."

"I suppose we could drive by. Although"—he cleared his throat—"it's not really part of my tour."

He ended up not only driving by but stopping and taking her in. Secretly, he was proud of his sister's house and pleased finally to be able to show it off to someone other than Ray Hu, and he thought Heidi would be impressed. She was polite but by no means awestruck, which disappointed him, until he remembered that, of course, Gary and Sherri were loaded, not to mention the grandma. The girl was used to fancy houses.

"Your room," Heidi said. "You haven't shown me your room."

"Not much to show," he muttered. "It's probably . . ." He was about to say "a mess" but, remembering how Pam had used the word to describe Heidi's father, stopped short.

He led her downstairs.

"Mmm, what's that I smell . . . ?" She inhaled. "What is it? Christmas trees? Your room smells like Christmas."

He nodded.

She walked around, picking up artifacts, inspecting them briefly, putting them back down gently. He tried to look at his room through her eyes and saw that it had zero character or personality, nothing distinctive, except for the smell of his Christmas tree soap; it merely looked like the guest room it had been designed to be. He didn't own many books besides the few he bought at garage sales; they were one of the only things Willa didn't buy him. She stuck mostly to things that would "enhance his image"—namely, clothes. His walk-in closet was crammed with clothes that he'd worn once or never, all bought by Willa, who tried to dress him like a contemporary Ken doll.

Heidi picked up the two foam-rubber ping-pong paddles on his dresser. They were identical except for the color: the green one was his; the blue, Willa's.

"Do you play?" she asked.

"Do I play," he said. "Oh, yes. How about you?"

"I'd kill you, honey."

"Ha-ha-ha. Oh, Heidi, no. No. You wouldn't. I guarantee you."

"All right, I challenge you. Let's find out. You have a table?"

"Unfortunately," Biff said, "my sister has her sweaters drying on it. She always has her sweaters drying on it. But it's just as well. I'd hate to embarrass you."

Heidi merely flicked her eyebrows up once, rather snootily, and looked around the room, tapping one of the paddles against her palm. "You don't have much, Biff, but what you have is very high quality. Can I see your high-school annual from last year?" she asked.

"My what?" His face went red.

"Your yearbook."

"What for?"

"Just because."

"You don't want to see that."

She smiled. "Don't worry, I won't read the signatures."

Two minutes later, incredibly, he was handing it over to her. She sat on the edge of his bed, fingering her French braid, flipping through, page by page.

Slowly she raised her face to him, amazed.

"Biff. You don't *have* any signatures."

He nodded.

"Poor unpopular boy," she said, and then laughed. Biff was relieved to see her laugh about it, and he laughed too and then immediately shook his head. He reached down and removed a long strand of blond hair from Heidi's sweatshirt. She didn't seem to notice.

Holding the yearbook on her lap, she located his own clownish picture. "Biff, you look about fourteen," she said. Then she looked up Tommie Isaac's picture and studied it somberly.

Biff looked at it over her shoulder. "It really isn't a good picture of her," he said.

"They never are," Heidi said, stroking her lips contemplatively with the side of her index finger. "She's not what I pictured."

"They never are," he said.

They left shortly after that, bringing along with them the two ping-pong paddles, which they decided to use that evening at the Kobleskas' clubhouse.

Next stop on the tour, Forest Ridge Park. By now it was raining harder. They got out and walked through the pink cherry blossoms, which the rain had piled on the ground like wet confetti. The play area was deserted; they each hopped on a swing. Heidi kept her legs straight out in front of her with her ankles together, watching her feet. Biff watched them, too.

"I'd like to see her house," she said.

"Whose house?"

"Hers."

"Tommie's? What for?"

She dismounted in mid-swing, landing on her feet in the sand, and started walking to the car.

Ten minutes later, he was driving by Tommie's house. He turned around and drove past it a second time.

"Stop," Heidi said.

He pulled over to the curb, half a block down from her house, the same spot he'd parked in yesterday afternoon.

"Okay," Heidi said, "go up and knock on her door. I'll wait here."

Biff laughed, or pretended to.

"I'm serious," she said. "I dare you. Go up there and get it over with. I'll sit here and read one of your books. Don't shake your head." She reached out and placed her hand on his shoulder. "Go on."

He looked at her hand on his shoulder, then up the street at Tommie's pink front door. For a second he almost did it. But he shook his head.

She removed her hand. "Okay. Then I'll do it."

"Do what?"

She opened her door and got out.

"Heidi, you're not going up there." He got out of his car and stood with his hands on the wet roof, watching her.

"Heidi! Come on!" He would have run up to her and tackled her, but he didn't want to make a scene in front of Tommie's house.

Shaking with rage, he got back in the car and drove past Heidi just as she was turning up the walkway. She had to be bluffing. She wouldn't really do it. He drove on up the street to Brookdale Elementary, pulling into the empty parking lot, hating himself but not exactly sure why. He wanted to get out and lock himself in the trunk and die, except that he wouldn't have fit, so he got out and stood in the rain instead. The rain calmed him. He grimaced, as if to cry, but couldn't produce any tears.

After a while, Heidi came up the street, hands in her pockets, hood up, walking slowly. She drifted by him, showing no expression. He followed her through the parking lot and onto the school grounds. Most of the window shades of the classrooms were pulled down, but Heidi found a window with the shade up and peered in, pressing her forehead against the glass and cupping her hands around her eyes.

"Heidi."

"Look, it's the library. Oh my."

She stood on her toes, peering in at Miss Jennings's library. When she finally turned around, she had tears in her eyes.

"What's the matter?" he asked. "What happened back there? Was she home? Why're you—"

"Oh be quiet!"

She walked away from him and sat down on a bench outside the cafeteria. It wasn't under shelter and the bench was wet, but Biff sat down next to her anyway.

"It's such a bleak day," she said. "I should *not* have gone by my house. That was a bad start. And then to see a library like that . . . it's like paradise. Don't you want to just live there, Biff, in that library? And back at Tommie's house, I knocked on the door and her mother answered. She was so incredibly nice. She was wearing an *apron*, can you imagine? And holding one of those things, one of those—what do you call them? My mother used to hit me with one."

He stared. "Rolling pin?"

"No, no. You know, for baking."

"Spatula?"

"Yes, yes, a spatula."

"Your mother used to . . . ?"

"Yes, didn't yours? Funny word for such a torture weapon. My mother had her good points, don't get me wrong. But . . . oh! Let me tell you about Tommie's father—"

"*Why* did you go to Tommie's house?"

"To see Tommie, of course. And her parents. But her father! Did you know he has a crew cut? He was doing something fatherly, I don't even know what, fixing something. He was using tools. And then I see this *library*. It's enough to make you . . . Where are my cigarettes?"

"In the car. Was she—was she there?"

"Oh yes."

"You saw her?"

"I saw her."

"You talked to her?"

She nodded.

"What did you say, Heidi? Tell me everything."

"Why? You don't deserve it, coward."

"Heidi, come on. Tell me what you said."

She closed her eyes and smiled up at the sky, at the rain, reminding Biff of some 1960s flower child with a wet French braid, and then she got up from the bench and started back toward the car. The rain came down even harder. Biff sat there watching her, feeling the water soak through the seat of his pants.

Biff climbed in behind the wheel. He and Heidi both sat there dripping.

"You're not going to tell me?" he finally asked.

"Now, don't ask questions, okay? I'll tell you when I'm

ready. Let's just sit and listen to the rain awhile. What does it sound like to you? What does it remind you of?"

He listened for a moment and shrugged. "I don't know. Kind of a crackling. Rice Krispies. Or Rice Chex. I don't know, I'm not good at things like that. What about you."

She smiled and nestled her head back against the seat. A drop of water ran down her face. "When I lived with my mom and dad, I'd lie in bed at night, and I could hear my dad in the next room typing on his word processor. It reminded me of rain on a tin roof."

Smiling, she shut her eyes. This gave Biff the chance to look at her face. He'd never really had a chance to study a girl's face. At least he couldn't remember doing so. Imagine being intimate enough with a girl to actually have the freedom to study, at leisure, her ear, neck, knee, toe, and so on. Her complexion was so smooth it was like . . . like fine china. He wasn't used to such a clear, creamy complexion; Tommie's was freckly, but then Tommie's existed only from distances, and in his dreams. Tommie didn't seem real, not compared to what he was seeing now; here was a real, touchable face, and so close to perfect—and *real*. Was it real?

He leaned back and sighed. Oh boy. He had a lot to learn, a long, long way to go in life.

But rather than depress him as this thought usually did, it suddenly hit him that life was, if anything, full of potential.

Heidi opened her eyes and caught him grinning at her.

"You're a madman," she said. "You do know that."

He nodded. "Oh, sure."

The sun came out, the tour continued. He showed her some touristy sights, which included thirteen views from

Queen Anne Hill, the salmon-viewing window at the Hiram Chittenden Locks in Ballard, the train tracks at Carkeek Park, where a kid was said to have gotten squashed, the fountain (turned off) at the UW campus, the illuminated stained-glass window (turned on) in the Burke Museum, Mertz's double-decker driving range, the run-up-your-leg squirrels of Woodland Park, several ducks, and, saving his best for last, he took her to his "all-time favorite bookshop," which, much to his shock and horror, had gone out of business three months ago and been replaced by a heavy-metal T-shirt shop called Drive On, Dude!

They went to the waterfront and bought a bag of french fries at a fish-and-chips carryout place, took it out on the pier, leaned against the railing, ate three fries, and tossed the rest, one by one, to the diving sea gulls. Biff enjoyed watching her more than the gulls.

"What are you looking at?" she asked, glancing at him and self-consciously touching her French braid.

"Nothing. What now?"

"I don't know. Let's do anything. I'm having fun. You're not as boring as you look."

"I know how to give a tour," Biff said, nodding and blushing after he'd said it.

"Let's go bowling," she said. "I do believe that's one of the things you guaranteed I wouldn't kill you at."

So they went to the Earl of Nottingham Lanes. He introduced her to Buildup.

"My old flame," he said, admiring the pinball machine even as his paw crept into his pocket in search of a quarter. "She still gives me a little spark."

"I'm so jealous," Heidi said.

"Heidi, let's play a couple of games on her. I can show you—"

"Go play with yourself, pervert." She walked away.

They got a lane and rented shoes. Biff found his lucky ball, number 355; Heidi took much longer finding the ball she wanted, and came back with two. She'd alternate.

While they were bent over putting on their bowling shoes, Biff suddenly remembered she hadn't paid him back for the cigarettes.

"Hey," he said.

"What?"

"Nothing."

He watched her take a few warm-ups. She was amazingly graceful and well coordinated, especially the way she followed through, her right hand finishing high above her head and her left shooting back. She was intense. Feeling his own competitive instincts awaken, Biff seemed to be having trouble with his footwork. He thought about the placement of his right foot and the six-inch slide of his left but then told himself, Don't think so much. He could beat this girl. Oh, how he wanted to beat her. Pretend she's Ray Hu, he told himself. But it was hard to pretend she was Ray Hu, or even Ray Hu's sister.

She won all three games. It left him feeling extremely bitter and surly, and he went and stood next to Buildup for solace, until Heidi came along and linked her arm through his and offered to buy him a hamburger at a place of his choice.

He chose an overpriced hamburger place in a shopping mall, about as far the other extreme from Grig's as you could get. No dead flies or glass ashtrays or one-armed men; it had a shiny pink Cadillac suspended from the ceiling, twenty-six kinds of hamburgers, waiters and waitresses who wore khaki shorts and informed you of their first names, and cushy comfortable booths. In the booth to Biff's back, facing Heidi, a little kid was playing peekaboo with Heidi. Biff hated it when strange kids played peekaboo with you at restaurants, but it was almost worth it, to see Heidi smiling in that soft, natural way he'd seen earlier in the Brookdale parking lot.

"Tell me now," he said.

"Tell you what?"

"What happened at Tommie's."

"No."

"All right then, tell me what you did to get suspended from school for two weeks."

"I told the vice principal to go fu—" She smiled at the kid, leaned toward Biff, and lowered her voice to a whisper. "I told him to go do to himself what his wife won't let him do to her."

Biff had to think about this for a second.

"Why?" he asked.

"Why did I tell him that? A long, ongoing feud between us, really too boring to even talk about."

The kid started to throw a fit when its mother tried to drag it away.

"Wave byebye," Heidi said to Biff, but he pretended to be studying the twenty-six different hamburgers on the menu.

Heidi pulled out a cigarette, but even before she could light up, a smiling waiter ("Alexander") pointed apologetically to a big sign that said: OURS IS A SMOKE-FREE ESTABLISHMENT.

For a second, Biff thought Heidi was going to give Alexander the same advice she'd given her vice principal, but she took another look at the sign and postponed her Nows for later.

"*Now* what are you grinning at?" she demanded.

He shook his head and tried to stop grinning, but didn't quite succeed.

CHAPTER ELEVEN

"**H**ow conveniently sexist," Lynn Kobleska said, twisting the cap off another bottle of beer—*pfflit*. "Females in the kitchen preparing the meal, while the men"—he held up his beer and contemplated it before taking a swig—"grease their wheels. Way it should be, huh, Beef? Sure I can't entice you to join me? I promise I won't tell Pamela. Ah, that's right. Last of the Teenage Mutant Teetotalers, aren't you?" Amazingly, Lynn seemed to think that was funny. He burped resonantly. "Has not been a good week, Beefer. Has not been a good month. And the year thus far, as a whole, has sucked." He tipped his head back and chugged.

They were standing in the living room, and as usual when he'd had a few, Lynn crowded up close to Biff, invading Biff's personal bubble with his beer-breath belches.

"You look *pallid*, Schmurr," Lynn said. "Like Death

with rosy cheeks. You ever get out and *do* anything, man? When was the last time you and I played chess?"

"New Year's Eve."

"New Year's Heave. Gad, is that all we did on New Year's Heave, is play chess? Who plays chess on New Year's Eve? Who in his right—come, fellow." He swung out at Biff and Biff ducked—after a few beers, Lynn often wanted to slap-box. But Biff realized Lynn was just motioning him to follow. "Something I want to show you in my study, Boof. No one, not even Pamela, has seen it yet."

They went into his study and closed the door.

"No wenches allowed in here," Lynn said. "How's that for hearty man-talk, huh? That is what—that is what law school does to you, my friend, reduces you to—gad, Schmurr, lighten up!"

The east and north walls of Lynn's study from floor to ceiling were lined with books. A stepladder leaning against the wall was used to reach the higher books. The other two walls were dark walnut paneling. On Lynn's huge desk, next to his computer, was a framed picture of a younger, longer-haired Pam in shorts, holding a steelhead trout, smiling and squinting into the sun. The chessboard that Biff and Lynn used was set up on a smaller table in front of the fireplace. Law books, most of them open, were strewn all over the floor. Lynn's two tennis rackets were leaning against the wall, next to his guitar, still in its case.

A framed sign in Pam's calligraphy hung on one paneled wall. It read: "A true poet's lips are touched with honey."

On the other wall, a bronze plaque dated two years ago:

Lynn had been one of the most popular teachers in Biff's high school, and Biff had had him for sophomore English comp, the year Lynn had won the award. But Biff hadn't voted for him; he hated it when teachers brought their guitars to class and strummed them while students were doing writing assignments. It had been awfully strange addressing this old family friend as "Mr. K." Lynn was a natural-born teacher; he'd gotten the teaching job his first year out of college, and as far as Biff knew, being an English teacher was the only thing Lynn had ever wanted to do. He had given it up last year when he was accepted to law school.

Thermal, the orange cat, squirted out from under Lynn's rump as he sat down in his high-backed leather chair behind the desk. Biff stayed standing and wished he were in the kitchen, slicing bread with Heidi.

"Ahhhh," Lynn said, settling himself in the expensive chair. He opened a drawer and took out a piece of yellow legal-size paper folded six or seven times into a small, tight cube. Biff knew instantly what it was.

"Here it are, Beefer. Composed last week in my car. I am reduced to writing poetry in my car during study breaks. And trips to the third-floor men's room of the law library, second stall from the left."

Thrusting the chunk of paper at Biff, Lynn finished his beer and stood up. "I'll leave you for a moment. While I go pay homage to the Porcelain Goddess."

He picked up the cat with one hand and carried it out, closing the door behind him.

Biff looked around the room. Lynn had it pretty good.

That chair alone would have cost Biff's father three months' salary when he was teaching. He unfolded the paper and smoothed it out against his chest. The dozen or so lines, in small pencil scrawl, roughly formed an hourglass.

Lynn used to bring his poems to school. His students would say, "Hey, Mr. K, got any new poems?" and Mr. K would look around sneakily and reach into his pocket and extract one of his folded-up yellow cubes, slowly unfold it, and read it to the class.

Once, at the beginning of one of the school-wide assemblies, a section of sophomores had refused, for some reason, to rise for the National Anthem. When the band finished playing, Lynn hurried up to the microphone, practically knocking over the principal, and said how he thought it was rotten not to stand for the National Anthem, and how his grandfather had almost died escaping from Eastern Europe to come to America. Lynn's voice started breaking, and Biff and most of the student body had felt kind of embarrassed, but the speech had been effective.

Lynn came back carrying two more beers.

"They're in there talking about you, Barf. Some of it good, I think. I think Heidi likes you. Sure I can't interest you in one of these here doggies?" He opened a bottle and put the other down on the desk, but quickly picked it up and slid a law journal under it.

"Beef, you know that song 'Little Deuce Coupe'? You know it? It was an oldie even back when I was in high school. I tell you, that song produces in me a rather peculiar reflex. Whenever I hear it, I smell Coppertone suntan lotion. Which then reminds me of my first love affair, senior year—I was a slow starter, like yourself—

Connie Mikaletti. 'Sprung Connie,' I used to call her. Fastest typist in the whole—shhh! Hear that? What was that sound? Was that my body?"

"I don't think so, Lynn."

"Good. Speaking of—what were we speaking of? Oh yes, Sprung Connie and love and wenches and all that. Now, that blond vixen in the kitchen? Heidi? That drink of water—" Lynn burped, which seemed to throw him off whatever train of thought he'd been riding. "What was I going to tell you? Have I *ever* given you bum advice, man? Have I? Did I ever give your brother Wally bum advice? You are in no position to answer that. Nor is that sister of yours. But I am. Yeah, I gave Wally some bum advice. But that's not important today, because Wally and me, man, we had something, we had an *understanding*, you see, that you and that spinster sister of yours will never fathom. Okay? Now back to—oh yes, Heidi. That drink of water. What I'm saying is that she—Heidi"— he took another swig—"she's leaving in a matter of days. Going back to Spokane Friday."

"So?"

"So? So you're on spring vacation, man! Go for it! What've you got to lose? You've only got a few more days with her. Savvy? A few more precious days of this thing called *life*, man! She needs somebody like you, Beefer. And you need her! Don't blow it. Don't let her down. Little Deuce Coupe!"

There was a long silence after that. Biff could hear a low ferry horn outside. A strange memory came to him. He remembered how Wallace Jr. used to practice his putts on the living-room carpet. He'd lag six or seven golf balls toward some object and Biff would roll them back to him. Occasionally he'd let Biff take a few putts.

Their father would be sitting at the dining-room table correcting math papers, while their mother might be doing something she stopped doing after Wallace Jr. was killed, cooking or sewing or ironing, and Willa might be in her room playing music. Lynn would often come over. He and Wallace Jr. would laugh at jokes Biff couldn't understand. They'd take their shirts off and flex their muscles and let Biff press their rock-hard biceps and triceps. They'd hold their tanned stomachs taut and say, "Go on, Beef, give it your best shot," and Biff would slug their stomachs as hard as he could, first one and then the other, over and over, until his fists got sore.

"Well, Biff?" Lynn said, looking at him.

"Huh?"

"What've you got to say, man?"

Biff looked at Lynn. "Thanks for the advice, Lynn."

"No charge. One other thing. Do not let Heidi drive a car. Don't let her *near* a steering wheel. Gary tells me a ride with Heidi is tantamount to a front-seat ride in a death wagon. You hear what I'm saying?"

"Yeah, Lynn. Thanks."

Lynn nodded and laughed. "Schmurr! If you could see the look on your face right now!" He pointed at the poem. "You read it?"

Biff shook his head.

"Come on, Beef. Read the poem. *Imbibe* it."

"Lynn, I have a question."

"Yeah."

"Why are you in law school?"

Lynn stared at him for a moment and seemed to go slightly pale, but recovered his composure. "Well, because that's whar they larn ye to be one a' them thar lawyer fellas."

"Why don't you go back to teaching?"

"Huh? Because. I'm a-gonna be one a' them thar lawyer fellas."

"Why?"

"*Why*? Make lots of money, of course. Buy lots of Ess Aitch Eye Tee. So Pamela will be able to continue on in her present mode of . . . continuation. And Pamela's mother and brother will keep on giving us lots of goodies and treats. We live in luxury's lap. Pamela's mother and brother do not like teachers, Beef. They think teachers are scum. Much too common and vulgar. And poor. Not like them lawyer fellas. Now, you going to read my poem?"

"No, Lynn."

"What?"

"I can't."

"What?"

"I can't concentrate. Poetry's over my head. It's . . ."

Lynn looked up at the ceiling. "Not even going to try." He looked back at Biff and held out his hand. "Give it."

"I just—"

"Give it here and shut up."

Biff handed it back.

"I'll read it to you. Just *listen* to the words. Don't try to *think* about what it *means*. Just listen to the *sounds*. Listen to the music. Think about what the sounds *do* to you."

He began reading the poem aloud, but almost immediately, Pam called, "Guys, come and get it!" Lynn stopped mid-sentence, aimed a nasty glare at the door, cleared his throat, and began reading the poem again from the beginning.

Staring at the paneled wall, Biff did as Lynn had said;

he didn't think about the words, just listened to the sounds. The sounds made him think of death. He didn't know why, they just did. Death made him think of cemeteries, which made him think of Wallace rattling around in his coffin, and Biff pictured himself standing above the grave, with some decomposed form of Wallace down below, and he could only picture the whole thing in black and white, like a grainy B movie.

The night Wallace was killed, Biff remembered hearing a car in the driveway about midnight, and a loud knock at the door. He went to his window and looked out and saw a highway patrol car parked in the driveway. The next thing he knew, he heard a shriek. His mother's. The loudest, most piercing and hellish shriek he'd ever heard, and he had thought they must be arresting her, hauling her off to jail. He went out into the hall, determined to fight and die for her, but Willa came and put her arms around him and told him it had something to do with Wally, some kind of accident.

That scream.

He hadn't visited Wallace's grave since February. Lately he'd been thinking so much about Tommie Isaac and going on that hike that he'd forgotten how the simple act of standing at his brother's grave helped him collect his thoughts. It was the closest thing he knew to praying. Was it possible that he didn't need the hike after all? That all he needed was to spend an afternoon at the cemetery?

Lynn lowered the paper and looked at Biff with wide, staring eyes. His voice was almost a whisper.

"Now then, Biff. What did those sounds do to you? What did they make you feel?"

Biff stared at the paneled wall.

"Biff. What'd they do to you, man?"

Biff kept staring at the wall.

"Biff!"

"What."

"What'd they do to you?"

"Nothing."

"You're a liar, Schmurr."

Biff shook his head.

"Hell, Schmurr," Lynn said. "Hell. You know what your problem is? I'll tell you, man. It's going to sound corny, but I don't care. Ready? *You won't give anything of yourself.* To anybody. Got it? That's your problem. Okay? Ah, well. Let's eat."

CHAPTER TWELVE

The four of them sat at the kitchen table with the blue-and-white-checked table-cloth and the basket of sliced French bread and Pam's limp spaghetti and a jar (straight from the microwave) of Mrs. Leland's Five-Star Lo-Cal Spaghetti Sauce and a salad that had a white dressing with green specks, which Heidi had concocted in an old mayonnaise jar.

Lynn had switched to white wine. He held up the bottle and offered Biff a glass. Biff shook his head.

"Teenage Mutant Teetotaler!" Lynn said for the second time, looking around the table to see if anyone was laughing. He put the bottle down with a clunk. "Now, what was I saying? Was I saying something?"

"No one was listening," Pam said, half closing her eyes.

"I'll take you up on that offer," Heidi said. She had

finished off her cranapple juice and was holding out her empty glass.

Lynn reached for the bottle.

"Not on your life," Pam said. "Forget it."

"Yeah, kid," Lynn said, withdrawing his hand. "Not on my life."

"You guys have to be nice to me in my final hours," Heidi said. "Before I go back to the snake pit."

"Poor Heiders," Pam said unsympathetically, taking a sip of cranapple juice.

"Wine wouldn't help you face the snake pit anyway, my dear," Lynn said. "Nor will whining." He was the only one who laughed.

"You don't want to go back at all?" Biff asked. He remembered he wasn't supposed to mention her father's offer, and he figured this was a harmless enough question, yet Heidi put her fork down and looked at him like it wasn't.

"Not her favorite subject, Biffy," Pam pointed out.

Lynn was shaking his head. "Unbelievable. They spend the whole day together and he finally gets around to asking that. What'd you guys *talk* about all day?"

"Oh, lay off him," Pam said. "You've had enough to drink. Let's everyone ignore Lynn. Maybe he'll dissolve." She turned to Heidi. "I forgot to tell you, your father called today."

Heidi, who had picked up her fork, laid it down again carefully and kept her eyes on it. "Did he."

"Finally got around to returning your calls," Pam said. "Really, Heidi, I don't know why you even bother. He said to tell you tomorrow's best for him. Lynn or I can give you a lift to the ferry. I would *hope* he'd be able to pick you up on the other side, rather than making you hitchhike the twenty-five miles. That is," Pam went on, "if you go at all. You don't have to, you know."

"I know," Heidi said.

"You do what you need to do, though," Pam said, "in your 'final hours.' I thought you and I could go up to Vancouver Tuesday or Wednesday and do some shopping. I know you don't care all that much about shopping, but we can visit a few galleries, too. We'll have a nice dinner and stay overnight in the best hotel. And maybe hit Victoria the next day, and have tea and crumpets at the Empress. How's that sound?"

Heidi was inspecting her fingernails. "Perfect."

"I protest," Lynn said. "I do not think it's proper for an aunt to stay in a hotel room in a foreign country with a niece without the presence of the uncle."

"Are you still here?" Pam said. "I thought we zapped you."

"You know," Heidi said, still inspecting her fingernails, "maybe this isn't the best time to bring this up—again. But maybe I could just not go back at all. Gary and Sherri wouldn't care. They'd rejoice. Someone please tell me why I should go back at all."

"You're right," Pam said. "This isn't the best time to bring it up."

"I guess nobody wants me," Heidi said to her fingernails.

"Do I hear violins?" Lynn said. Then he winked at Biff.

Pam leaned toward her niece. "We'll go over it once more. It's not that we don't want you, kiddo." (The "kiddo" struck Biff as forced.) "We'd simply love to have you stay here with us. But you have to finish the school year there. Bite the bullet. It's only three more measly months, plus a few weeks of summer school to make up this thingy, this suspension. But you can come spend part of August with us. We insist. And, for heaven's sake, Gary and Sherri want you, you silly goose! You all just needed a time out from each other."

"We want you, Heiderooski," Lynn said, patting Heidi's lifeless, pinkish hand.

Pam, eyes on the hand-patting, ripped her bread in half. "Of *course* we do."

"I've been thinking about it more and more," Heidi said. "Just ditching high school completely. It's utterly stupid. I hate it. I don't know if I can take another three months—plus stupid summer school. Plus two years after that. I'm serious. I've been looking into my options. There are alternative schools in Seattle, and there's—Pam, listen—I can get my GED and then go on to community college. And work part-time. And I could do all the cooking and housework here for you guys. You could get rid of that housekeeper you have and save money."

"You'd be a dropout," Pam said flatly; only her hair remained perky. "We will not provide safe haven for a dropout. And we don't pay for the housekeeper, my mother does."

"Actually," Biff said, "I've heard of the—" But nobody understood him, because he had jammed a string of spaghetti into his mouth and was trying to bite it off. He swallowed. "I've heard of the GED. It's doable."

"I detest that word," Lynn said.

"It's a worthy goal," Biff said.

"Biff," Pam said, "how dare you encourage her!"

"It *is* a worthy goal," Heidi said. "Oh, Biff, you are so right for a change. Would you pass the bread, thank you. I could ace the GED right now, tomorrow. I'm not as stupid as I seem. I'm just a little shaky on fractions. I forget when to invert."

"We all do," Lynn said. "We all do!"

"This is all absurd," Pam said. "You have no reason to leave school. What's wrong with school?"

"Everything," Heidi said.

"Then that's your fault," Pam said, "because you only get out of school what you put into it, which for you is zero. You don't belong to any clubs or groups or involve yourself in any activities. You hang out with those—those self-centered bitches. Listen, kiddo, speaking as your mother's sister, I'm telling you, you're *going* to finish out the year and you're *going* to graduate in two years."

Heidi glared at her aunt.

"Hey, I didn't think you wanted to be away from old Richie Fitzwhosis," Lynn said.

"Will you please not mention his name," Heidi said, still looking at Pam.

"Beg pardon." Lynn made the sign of the cross. "Name not to be taken in vain," he said to Biff out of the side of his mouth.

"I really can't even fathom this GED business," Pam said. "I happen to believe in a good old-fashioned high-school diploma, and good old-fashioned finishing what you start, namely, school, whether it's boring or not. I was one of those people who did my assignments without complaining about needing to go out for—for cigarette breaks!"

"You were a cheerleader," Lynn said. "Cheerleaders are not of this realm. You lived on a different plane of existence. Still do, as a matter of—"

"That does it!" Pam picked a piece of celery out of her

salad and fired it at him—and not playfully; she had a good arm. "I've had it with you. I will not listen to you run down cheerleaders again."

"Knew that was coming, could have ducked," Lynn muttered, rubbing the red mark just below his left eye.

"Besides," Pam turned back to Heidi, "neither Gary nor my mother would ever go for any of this."

"Screw Gary," Lynn said, "and screw the Old Barracuda."

"Right," Pam said. "You tell them that. As they're handing you the checks that pay for your law school and your—"

"We all know what they pay for, Pamela, no need to announce it to the congregation. Screw their checks. And screw those two. And I'll tell 'em that. If Heidi wants to come live with us, let her. She doesn't need anyone's permission. I'll say that again, Pamela, because it's the law. She does not need anyone's permission. She could live with her father or with us or with—with old Beefsteak here, for that matter, though God only knows why she'd want to do that. And if Gary and the 'Cuda don't like it, they can take their croquet mallets and stuff them down each other's throats and I'll help 'em do it and I'll tell 'em that, too, right to their faces, if need be-eeeeeee." (He burped loudly on the last word.)

Nobody said much after that. Biff was the only one still eating.

The phone rang. Pam was gone quite a while, during which time Biff and Lynn watched Heidi sculpt what looked like a bird's nest out of her uneaten spaghetti. At one point Biff caught her eye and she gave him a quick smile, as if to acknowledge she knew he'd kept her secret. This made him feel good.

Pam came back with the phone.

"This is Gary. He's calling to see how we're getting along with Heidi. I told him you had a few words to say to him. Dear."

Lynn started to say something, then stopped and reached out. "Give me that there telephone thingy." He cleared his throat loudly and leaned back in his chair. "Gare! You scuzzball! I can smell you from here! How's it hangin', pard? . . . Huh? Yeah . . . Yeah . . . Huh? Oh, yeah, you know. You betcha . . . Hey, Gare, when're we going fishin'? . . . Yeah? . . . Yeah? . . . Hohohohohoho!"

Heidi got up quietly and left the table. Pam followed her. "Hey, Gare, listen up, pardo. Huh? Yeah, she's sitting right—oops, no, she isn't. She *was* here, but she snuck away on me, that little vixen! Huh? . . . Oh, ain't that the truth! Hahahahahahahahahahahahha! Reminds me of the one about the three lawyers and the iguana . . ."

Biff got up and left the table, too. He took his time walking down the hall toward the bedrooms. Heidi's door was partially open, and he hesitated as he came to it. Through the opening he saw Heidi sitting on the edge of her bed. Pam was sitting next to her. They were both looking at the floor, not saying anything.

Heidi noticed him and gave him a gentle smile. "Is he still telling Gary off?" she asked.

"Really letting him have it."

"You know what I feel like doing?" she said. "Creaming you at ping-pong, that's what. But first we have to help Auntie Pam clean up the kitchen."

"You sweet thing," Pam said.

CHAPTER THIRTEEN

Twenty minutes later they were riding the elevator, which smelled of Mrs. Leland's Five-Star Lo-Cal Spaghetti Sauce.

"Here," Biff said, extending the two ping-pong paddles. "I'll let you choose."

She took the choice seriously, inspecting and weighing both paddles. As the elevator opened at the ground floor, she handed him the blue paddle (Willa's) and kept the green (his). Wouldn't you know it.

"Uncle was acting a bit strange tonight," she said.

"Uncle has lost it," Biff said.

"You two had a long talk before dinner," she said, biting the paddle as they walked through the lobby.

"Yes we did. Don't leave teeth marks on that."

She removed the paddle from her teeth and gave her left palm a few whacks with it. "Anything I'd be interested in?"

"Maybe."

"Like?"

"Oh, Lynn read a poem to me. And we talked about you."

She smiled. "Did you. I'm so glad. What did you say?"

He stopped and looked at her as they came to the lobby exit. "I'll be glad to tell you. You tell me what happened at Tommie Isaac's house today."

Her smile broadened and she shook her head. They continued out the door, across the courtyard, past the outdoor swimming pool, to the clubhouse. Heidi had a key that let them in.

"Lynn said you were a drink of water," Biff said.

"What does that mean?"

"I have absolutely no idea."

There wasn't a soul in the clubhouse, although the TV had been left on and a pool cue left leaning against it. Biff walked over and turned the TV off.

They started warming up. She was quite good. Steady, defensive, putting strange spins on the ball. Good but beatable.

"Does Gary have a table?" Biff asked.

"Nope."

"You play often?"

"No. Rally for serve?"

"Let's warm up a little longer," he said. His backhand chip was not working: his wrist wasn't flicking the way it should. He took off his watch, even though it was on the other wrist.

"Ready yet?" she asked.

"No. But I'll go ahead."

She won the first game, 21–18.

They traded sides.

"I knew I needed more warm-up time," he said.

"Yes, Biff."

She won the second game, 21–16.

Biff had been chewing his lower lip and it was bleeding. He excused himself and went into the bathroom, where he had a quiet, controlled paroxysm of rage. Then he rinsed his face.

When he came out, she was sitting on the sofa smoking a cigarette, not far from the NO SMOKING sign on the wall above the TV.

He leaned on the table, looking at her, bouncing the ball up and down on his paddle. Smug. That was the word for her just now. Who *was* this girl?

"This third game," he said, "I might actually have to start trying."

"Yes, Biff."

"Heidi, if I don't beat you, I'll—I'll . . ."

"Careful," she said.

"You think you're unbeatable. But you're not. No one is."

"I told you, I just like to win. I expect it."

"Pride cometh before a fall."

She laughed.

He caught the ball with his left hand and pointed the paddle at her.

"You tell me. I have a right to know. What happened at Tommie's?"

The back of her head was resting on the sofa. She closed her eyes for a few seconds and then opened them. "I simply told her . . . oh, let's see, what did I tell her? I told her, 'Biff is an outstanding fellow, and he's outside sitting in his car, afraid to come up and tell you that he dedicated his essay to you. I'm afraid you'll have to call him up because he'll never do it. Somebody should, so it might as well be you.' Or something like that."

He laid his paddle gently on the table and sniffed. "You didn't say that."

"Something like that. I don't have it verbatim."

"You wouldn't do that to me. If I believed you really said that, I'd wring your neck."

"Look, Biff, it all turned out fine. You'll simply have to trust me."

"Trust you. I don't even *know* you."

She closed her eyes and sighed. "I'm suddenly tired. Tired, tired, tired. Thinking of going back to Spokane makes me tired. I wish you'd give me another good book like *Gatsby* to read. What's tomorrow, Sunday? I suppose you're too sick of me to want to see me tomorrow."

"You said it." He went over and picked up his watch. "It'll be Sunday in exactly forty-two minutes."

"Thank you, Biff."

He walked around and around the table, trying to analyze why, during the first two games, he had missed so many topspin slams to her backhand corner.

"Are you really sick of me?" she asked.

"Yes."

She blew lazy smoke rings up to the ceiling. "Because, I was wondering if you'd like to come with me and meet my father. You could drive. That way he wouldn't have to pick me up at the ferry."

"Overnight?"

She nodded.

He picked up his paddle and took a couple of swats at the air, pacing around the table. "You don't have any intention of going back to Spokane, do you."

"Why do you say that?"

"A feeling."

She shrugged. "It depends."

"On?"

"Certain things. How it goes with my father."

"Yes, I'd like to go," he said. "I was thinking I might go visit my brother's grave tomorrow. I need to do that. But I can do it early in the morning before I pick you up. Yes, I'd like to go with you."

She turned her head to look at him. "I could go with you. To your brother's grave."

"Oh, no, you wouldn't want to do that."

"Yes, I would. Unless it's the type of thing you'd rather do alone."

"Well, I've never done it with anybody else," he said, running his fingers through his wild hair. "Well, you could come along . . . I suppose. If you wanted to. I've never taken anyone to his grave. You'd be—you'd be the first. It's not like going to the park, Heidi. I mean, there aren't swings or anything."

"Biff, I think I know the difference between a cemetery and a park. You won't have to entertain me."

"It's just that, if I think you're bored it'll make me nervous and spoil the mood."

"You don't want me to come, fine."

"No, I do . . . If you really want to."

"I told you I do. We can catch the ferry afterward."

"Yeah . . ."

"Okay then?"

"I guess Wallace won't mind . . ."

"Well if you think he would . . ."

"No, no . . ."

"Let's rally for serve." She got up and went to the window and tossed out her cigarette.

Biff won the rally and served the first five points. At 2–3, Heidi serving, the door opened and Follett, the manager, appeared.

"Who's been smoking in here?"

"Some man," Heidi said. "With a barely noticeable limp. Or I mean lisp. Carrying a bag of Doritos. Do you remember which flavor, Biff?"

"No smoking allowed here," Follett said.

"We pointed that out to him," Heidi said. "Two-three, my serve."

"Lounge closed at eleven."

"We'll just finish this game," Heidi said. "We're playing for high stakes."

"The lounge closed at eleven."

Heidi raised her voice as if Follett were hard of hearing. "We're just going to finish our game."

"No. That's it. Lounge is closed."

Heidi lowered her paddle and looked at Follett. "Where does it say the lounge closes at eleven? Is there a sign posted?"

"If you don't leave I'm going to call Security."

"Why?"

"Because the lounge closed at eleven."

"Show me where it says that."

"I won't show you a dang-blasted thing. It's in the lease. Go look it up in the lease."

Heidi laughed. "You made that up!"

"Hah? You ain't even residents here. Neither one of you."

"What has that got to do with the hours of the lounge?" Heidi said. "Are you making up another rule now?"

"The lounge is closed."

"Who says?"

115

"I says."

"You just make up any old rule that pops into your head. You just don't like us."

"You were smoking."

"How dare you accuse me."

"I'm going to call Security!"

"Oh, go to bed."

Follett started to gasp and sputter.

Biff was afraid the old man was going to keel over. "Heidi, maybe we should just go."

"I *hate* it when people make up rules just because we're teenagers. I hate that."

"I'm calling Security!"

Follett hurried out the door.

"Two-three, my serve," Heidi said.

Biff didn't pick up his paddle. He stood looking across the table at her with his mouth slightly open.

"Two-three," Heidi repeated.

He picked up his paddle.

At 7–7, Lynn came walking in, yawning. His hair was rumpled and he was wearing a bathrobe and tennis shoes. His hairy legs were bare. Follett, who had come in behind him, said he wouldn't call Security if Lynn could get his niece to leave. Lynn spoke to the old man in a calm, soothing voice. The subject of the lease came up. Mr. Follett was persuaded to go and get a copy of it. It said something about residents and guests of residents being welcome to use the clubhouse for social purposes between the hours of 9 a.m. and midnight. After midnight, they needed to obtain special permission from the manager.

Heidi had won. There was that smug, triumphant look

again. Biff was actually disappointed. Didn't she ever lose?

By now, however, it was eight minutes to midnight. Follett, who appeared exhausted, told them to turn off the lights whenever the hell they decided to leave, he didn't give a hang anymore, he was going to bed.

Heidi yawned. "I've had it, too. We'll have to finish our game another time. I'll see you in the morning, Biff." She linked her arm through Lynn's. "Come on, you, let's get you back to bed." She led him out of the lounge.

Biff stayed behind. After turning off the lights one by one, he stood in the darkness and silence. Thoughts of Heidi and Tommie and Wallace Jr. and Willa and himself all swam around in his head in a jumble. He thought, with a certain amount of wonder: These have been the two fullest days of my life.

CHAPTER FOURTEEN

The day wasn't quite over. Biff got home at 12:25 and was glad to find Willa waiting up for him in the kitchen. It was nice being waited up for once in a while. He sat down at the kitchen table and stared at his sister's cat-of-the-month wall calendar.

Willa brought him the paper, skimpy on Saturdays, and asked if he'd like a bowl of cereal. He shook his head; his routine was too disrupted for his usual bowls of cereal.

Willa, who rarely sat when she did anything, went back to the counter next to the sink, held her bowl of Frosted Mini Wheats just below her chin, and chewed rapidly. She was barefoot, wearing a spinsterish button-down wool sweater over a knee-length T-shirt. Her knobby knees stuck out. Her thin bare calves, the color of nonfat milk, seemed almost translucent.

"Seeing her tomorrow, too? Bippy, this is serious!"

"I'm taking her to visit her father."

"Really? You get to meet the mysterious Marc Hamilton? Now, *that* should be interesting."

"What do you know about him, Willa?"

"Not a whole lot. He lives over on one of the islands."

"What else?"

"Well, he wrote that novel. He spent years and years writing it and almost nobody read it. But then they made it into a movie, not long after Kim died, and the movie did very well, incredibly well, and the book went into paperback and did almost as well as the movie."

"But what's he like?"

"I don't know, I never met him. Pam hardly knows him, either. She says he used to be very handsome and charming."

"Used to be? Before Kim died?"

"I suppose."

"Pam said he's a mess. A *mess*. What do you think she means by that?"

"His life, I suppose."

"But in what way?"

"Biffy, I really wouldn't know. Maybe because he lives in a trailer."

"A *trailer*?"

"Yes."

"Good Lord." Biff shuddered. "He parks it on his estate?"

"His what?"

"I thought he lived on an estate?"

"Who told you that?"

"He *doesn't?*"

"Pam's never said anything about an estate. I think she would have."

Biff closed his eyes and shook his head. "Oh boy. I should've known. Does he work?"

"I don't think he does much of anything, Biffy. You'll have to see for yourself, I guess."

"A *trailer* . . . Why did he stop writing? Because Kim died?"

Willa shrugged. "That's something you'll have to find out, too."

"What was Kim like?"

"Oh! Beautiful, crazy, rebellious . . . wild." (There was that word again.) "Completely the opposite of Pam and Gary. Pam said they had some nickname for her in high school—the Fiery Italian or something. I met her a few times. She was incredible! You know the actress Sophia Loren? Kim looked exactly like her. It was uncanny. But I guess you'd have to say she lived a real turbulent life, you know? Excessive. Like an artist or rock star, only without the . . . focus. No special focus. Like Pam has her art, and Gary has his business. But Kim, she was just wild. Just bound to die young. And that's what she did. That's really all I know. She had guts. She was the only one who wasn't afraid to stand up to their mother, and I admire her for that. *Nobody* stands up to the old lady. When Kim ran off with Marc Hamilton, her mother disowned her. Completely and totally."

"How did she die?"

"She was drunk and she drove her car into a telephone pole."

"Marc wasn't hurt?"

"Marc wasn't with her."

"She was alone?"

"I think so, Biffy."

"Which telephone pole?"

"I have no idea."

"Where did it happen?"

"I don't know. An intersection."

"Which one?"

"Which intersection? Biffy . . ."

"In Seattle?"

"Yes."

"What'd they do with Heidi?"

"The old lady took her. Marc Hamilton didn't fight it. I don't know whether he signed legal papers or what. He had no money at the time, no job. His book had sold about two copies. Speaking of money, Bippy, how much have you got? You're going to need some for the ferry. I'll go get my purse."

"I'd better get a job," he said.

"Oh, not right now." She disappeared through the doorway and came back with her purse and his wallet.

"Willa, you can't just keep handing me money."

"Sure I can. I like handing you money. I like taking care of my baby brother."

"Your brother the parasite."

"Oh, Bippy."

He watched her stuff money into his wallet.

"Willa? Do you ever think about Wallace?"

"Sure."

"Why don't you ever go visit his grave?"

"Because it's just a grave. Wally's not there."

"Yes he is."

"No he isn't."

"Yes he is."

"No he isn't, Biffy."

"Who's there, then? Who's there?"

"Biffy, calm down. You know what I mean. It's just bones."

"Wallace's bones."

"Biffy, I don't want to get into this. You know what I mean. There was more to Wally than flesh and bones."

"Sure there was. But that's all that's left of him now—"

"I want to know what day next week I can invite Heidi over for dinner."

"Who cares."

"Oh stop it. Stop it." She tipped her cereal bowl back for the last gulp of milk and rinsed the bowl in the sink.

"Willa?"

"More questions?"

"No. I'm going to bed. Willa, for my own good, don't give me any more money. I just take and take. You make things too easy for me. I need to learn responsibility."

"You have plenty of time to learn responsibility. What you need right now is a social life. That costs."

"What about *your* social life?"

"It's perfectly merry."

"I could move out and get a place of my own next year."

"Oh, don't be such a downer. Life's too short."

"Yeah, it sure was for Wallace."

Willa clamped her mouth shut.

"All right, Willa." He rubbed his eyes. "Good night."

"Night, Bippy."

He stood up, but sat back down. "Willa?"

"Yes?"

"Why don't you marry Paul and settle down?"

"Because I don't want to marry Paul."

"Why not? Because he works in a supermarket?"

"Of course not."

"I think if you married Paul you'd have a happy life."

"I have a happy life now."

"Then why are you always reading those self-help books?"

"Self-improvement, Biffy, not self-help. They keep me focused. I'm happy with who I am, but I know I can be better."

"Better in what way? Richer?"

"Sure. But other ways, too."

"What ways? Name a couple. Spiritual ways?"

"Biffy, stop interrogating me."

"What ways?"

"Achieving my goals. I've got a series of specific, well-defined goals that I've set out to systematically—"

"But why, Willa? Why all these goals?"

"Because that's what life is all about, Biffy. Setting goals and striving for them."

"No." Biff shook his head. "No, Willa."

"No what?"

"That's not what life's all about."

"All right then, what's it about, Biffy. You tell me."

Rubbing his tired face, Biff continued to shake his head.

"Come on, I'm waiting, Biffy. Tell me."

"It's not goals . . ."

"Then what is it?"

"I don't know."

"Eating cereal and hanging around Wally's grave? Is that it, Biffy?"

"I don't know." He stood up. "All I know is, you should marry Paul. That's all I know. Good night, Willa."

His sister smiled. "Good night, Bippy."

CHAPTER FIFTEEN

Sunday morning was a rerun of Saturday. Once again, Biff waited in the Kobleskas' living room, this time sipping a grapefruit juice, while the rain spattered the picture window and Pam rousted her niece out of bed. Eventually Heidi came out, wearing the same white-loop earrings from yesterday, but a different hairstyle.

"You let your French braid down," he said.

"How observant. Your hair looks funnier than usual today."

"Oh?"

He suddenly remembered he'd forgotten to shower this morning. Strange. He'd left without so much as a glance in the mirror.

"But who cares about hair," Heidi said. "Especially when you're visiting your brother's grave."

"Well put," he said.

Like yesterday, she wanted coffee. He drove to the Lucky 4 U but was disappointed to find that it was closed Sundays. That old man, he thought, had better start keeping up with the times. He can't compete with these twenty-four-hour places.

Driving away from the store, Biff felt sure that he would have passed his test this time; he would have exuded kindness and goodwill right into the old man's sour kisser.

Yeah, sure. But why did it matter? Why the test? Why this need to do Good? He knew it didn't have anything to do with "achieving whatever he desired," as he had read in Willa's book. But it did have something to do with what Lynn had said last night, about "giving himself." That was it. That was love. It tied in with his nightly reading of the newspaper, too. Call it a sense of belonging. And his occasional visits to garage sales and other such things—these also gave him a sense of belonging. Belonging to what? Well, to the human race.

He pulled into a twenty-four-hour place just up the street, where the clerk didn't give him a bad time and the coffee was freshly brewed and dispensed from a silver thermos that had a smiling face on it, and the orange juice was so cold you could hear ice chips clink when you shook it, but he opted instead for a pint of chocolate milk and five dollars' worth of gas. Heidi sat in the car sipping her coffee while Biff pumped the gas.

The cemetery was seventeen miles north of Seattle, at the end of a winding road that went through a suburban, residential area. The office and mausoleum came first. Then, farther up the road, you took a left through a pair of black iron gates.

The green rolling hills, interspersed with trees, would

have made a nice par 3 golf course. Curbless lanes, just wide enough for a car, coursed through the grounds.

At the center, the highest point of the cemetery, stood a ten-foot-tall white stone statue of a shepherd. At night it was lit up from the ground by a circle of floodlights. From the perimeter road, glimpsed through the trees, it looked like a huge glowing ghoul stalking the graveyard. Up close in daylight it wasn't quite so spooky. The index finger of its right hand had been snapped off by some vandal. It had no eyes, just blank sockets, and its arms groped out in front of it like a sleepwalker's. On second thought, it was pretty scary even up close in daylight.

The speed limit was a creeping ten, but Biff was going about five. The deeper they drove into the cemetery, the more somber and overcast the sky grew. Biff wondered what Heidi was thinking. Something to do with her mother, maybe, or the upcoming visit to her father, or both?

"Your mother's, uh . . . buried in Spokane?" he asked.

She shook her head no.

Maybe he shouldn't have mentioned her mother. Not here and now.

After a pause she said, "Her ashes are floating in Puget Sound. They were the only thing of hers my dad kept. He scattered them off a ferry."

Biff pulled over next to a tree and cut the motor. They sat for a minute in silence. Single drops from the tree limbs above plopped onto the car, amid the soft, steady rain.

Heidi took the umbrella she'd borrowed from Pam, Biff put on his baseball cap, and they started off among the headstones and the small square bronze plaques. Biff walked with his eyes lowered but he could feel Heidi next to him. Eventually he stopped at the plaque bearing his brother's name and the pair of dates that had sandwiched his brother's life. Rain beaded up on the letters and made tiny splashes. Biff felt the rain on the back of his neck. It began to soak through his cap. Drops dripped down the bill. All he heard was the gentle tapping of the rain on his cap and leaves and grass and headstones, rain everywhere. His hands made cold fists in his pockets.

What would be left of his brother down there by now? Just bones? What had happened to the life that had been inside of Wallace? The integrity, grace, purpose that had belonged only to Wallace? Where had they gone?

Biff raised his face to the rain and inhaled the fresh, moist air. Heidi was no longer beside him; she was standing off a ways with her umbrella on her shoulder, looking at a headstone.

Last night in the lounge and later while driving home, Biff had wondered whether he was making a mistake bringing her here. Could he trust her? What if she did something to spoil the mood? Lit up a cigarette or acted impatient to leave? Something to shatter the peace? He looked over at her profile. She made a still picture, except for the umbrella, which she slowly twirled. From this distance, her eyes appeared to be closed. Her lips seemed to be moving.

He was glad she'd come.

From the cemetery they headed north to the ferry terminal in Mukilteo. Biff told their destination to the booth person, paid the hefty round-trip fare, and joined the line of waiting cars, all sitting with engines off. Heidi lit a cigarette and rolled her window down halfway and used the parking lot as an ashtray. More cars lined up behind them.

Two cars ahead, Biff noticed a yellow school bus. It took him a few moments to realize that it was filled with senior citizens. On the back of the bus a hand-painted sign read: CHA CHA DANCE CLUB. The thought of these old people riding a school bus and dancing gave him the creepies. A few of them, those who could walk or who didn't mind the rain or weren't afraid of stumbling on the steps and breaking their hip, got out of the bus to stretch their whatevers. They were all wearing blue windbreakers that read on the back: CHA CHAS GET THE MOST OUT OF LIFE.

He turned to Heidi. "Did you know Cha Chas get the most out of life?"

She was staring into space.

He drummed his fingers on the steering wheel for a while and noticed that the calluses on his pinball-flipper fingers were softening up. He plucked a few hairs from his eyebrows. He drummed some more.

Then he turned to Heidi again. "So, you really think you might quit school?"

"Will you do me a favor?"

"Sure."

"Don't ask boring questions today."

"All right."

They sat quietly. The rain came down and cars continued to line up.

After a few minutes Heidi turned her body to face him, her back against the door.

"Biff, do you have a best friend?"

"Sure."

"Who?"

"Who? Ray Hu."

"Ray Hu . . . Is Ray Hu a nerd?"

"Ray Hu is a heck of a guy."

"What's he doing now?"

"Today? Nothing."

"How old is he?"

"What?"

"How old is he."

"Ray Hu? Why do you ask?"

"Why is your face turning red?" she asked, smiling. "You're blushing! Now, why would you be blushing? How old is Ray Hu?"

Biff looked at her. "If you must know, he's a year younger than you are."

"Ah, your best friend's fourteen and you're embarrassed. That's cute. Don't be ashamed of your best friend."

"I'm not ashamed. He's a heck of a guy."

"So you said."

"Ray Hu is—Ray Hu is the kind of guy who'd lay down his life for you. A lot of people say they would, but he'd do it."

"Would you lay down your life for him?"

"I like to think I'd lay down my life for anybody. For a stranger. I probably wouldn't, but I like to think it."

Heidi tossed her cigarette over her shoulder out the window, keeping her eyes on him but not saying anything.

"What about you?" he asked, looking at the dashboard. "Are you Miss Popularity in your high school?"

"You said you wouldn't ask boring questions."

"Sorry . . . Who's your best friend?"

"I have three. Two I hate, and one I can't stand."

He looked at her. "Your best friends? How can you hate your best friends?"

"Easy."

"Huh," he said. "Three best friends."

"Yes. Their names, in alphabetical order, are Fawn, Kirby, and Danielle."

"That's not alph—"

"I went by their last names."

"Is Fawn a boy or a girl?"

She laughed. "Why, Biff, that's the first funny thing you've said on purpose. Congratulations."

"Thank you." He wasn't aware he'd tried to be funny.

"They're all girls," she said. "Fawn is my doubles partner."

"Doubles . . . as in tennis?"

She nodded. "We—that is, Gary, Sherri, and Gran— we all belong to a tennis club. A snobby, exclusive, prejudiced club. I hate it. It's a perfect symbol of my life in Spokane: shallow, self-centered, mindless. It's very much like my high school. Everybody busy trying to impress everybody else. And that, Biff, is something I like about you."

"What?"

"You would not fit into my life back home."

She stretched her legs out straight and rested her tennis shoes, damp and grassy from the cemetery, on his lap and put her left hand on top of the seat, which gave Biff the opportunity to study her hand, her fingers, the rings on them.

"You know something, Heidi?"

She smiled. "What's that, Biff?"

"I haven't thought of Tommie for several hours."

"What makes you think of her now?"

"I don't know. Your rings, I guess. They suddenly reminded me you're a girl. I have a girl sitting in my car."

"Oh Biff, you are so junior-high."

"Yeah, that's me," he said, nodding. "You said it."

It began to rain hard, as an attendant, with her hood up, waved them up the ramp and onto the ferry. They started to get out of the car amid rumbling engines and squealing tires and slamming car doors. By instinct Biff grabbed a book. "Bad luck not to take one of these with you on a boat," he told Heidi. "In case of shipwreck."

He offered her one, but she shook her head and held up her cigarettes. "Bad luck not to take these."

Biff made sure he had his keys before he shut his own door. Once, when he was a kid, he saw a man who had accidentally locked his keys in the car on a ferry. It had not been a pretty sight.

They climbed the steep, narrow stairway to the deck. Heidi went straight to the snack bar and stood in line. Biff looked around. It had been years since he'd set foot on a ferry, and he was shocked to find they now had a couple of old video games. Video games on a ferry! He shook his head in disgust. At the same moment, his hand was crawling around in his pocket for a quarter.

Heidi came back with a Styrofoam cup of coffee. She gave him a sip and he cringed because it had no cream or sugar.

"Don't you dare play a video game," she said.

"Wouldn't think of it."

"What were you fishing around in your pocket for, hm?" she asked, smiling.

"Merely scratching an itch. Pinball's my thing, Heidi,

not video games. Let's go out on deck. You should've brought your umbrella."

"Bad luck on a boat," she said.

They went outside and leaned over the railing, watching the ferry pull away from the pier—it looked more like the pier was pulling away from the ferry. They were all alone on deck—the downpour of a moment ago was now just a mist. Biff put his paperback in his hip pocket. The brisk wind whipped Heidi's hair across her face and she shoved it back with one hand while taking a sip of coffee with the other. Her face glowed. Now and then she pressed her body ever so slightly against Biff's while pointing to some landmark ashore. The engines rumbled and the boat rocked slightly and everything, including Biff, vibrated.

They walked all the way around the boat, twice, and then went inside to take off their coats and hang them up to dry. In the large open area in the stern, the tables had been cleared away and a six-piece band had set up—clarinet, sax, trumpet, trombone, bass guitar, and a small drum set. The name of the band, painted on the bass drum, was CHICK AND THE SOPHOMORES. They were all wearing yellow vests and white shirts, except for the clarinetist, who wore a yellow shirt with a white vest that read *Chick* on the front of it.

"That's Chick on the licorice stick," Biff said. It was something his dad would say.

"Look!" Heidi said, her voice slightly tremulous. "They're all wearing *glasses*!"

True, although, unlike the vests, no two eyeglasses were the same. None of the Sophomores looked a day under sixty, except for Chick, who maybe squeaked under by a few days.

The Cha Cha Dance Club had taken off their blue windbreakers and were sashaying around the dance floor, putting on quite a spectacle for the ferry passengers. At first Biff thought he'd better hide his eyes from this pitiful sight, but pretty soon he had to admit these old folks weren't that bad. The men were doing all kinds of fancy struts and steps, and the ladies twirled and hopped around like sparrows. Each couple had its own unique style—some were loose and jazzy, others stiff and formal; some were smiling, others deadly serious. Not a single person fell down.

When the song ended, the Cha Chas applauded. Chick lowered his clarinet and said, "Well, howdy, all you boy and girl Cha Chas, and all you other fine ferry folk as well," and the Cha Chas said "Howdy" back. Chick chatted for a minute and then the band started playing another swing tune and the Cha Cha Dance Club went at it again, joined by some of the less inhibited ferry passengers.

Biff surprised himself at getting such a kick out of watching these sliding, scooting dancers. He kept glancing at Heidi, afraid she was getting bored or was about to say something derisive or sarcastic. But she turned to him and smiled and said, "Biff, don't you love this?"

"Don't you?"

"Don't *you*?" Her smile was radiant. Simply radiant. "Biff, let's dance!"

He shook his head. "Pure spectator sport."

But soon enough an old man came along and whisked Heidi onto the dance floor. She looked a little wooden at first, trying to follow the man's steps; she seemed to take it almost as seriously as her bowling or ping-pong. Two songs later, she'd loosened up and was getting the hang of it. Between songs Chick said, "I see old Jim Howard's found himself a perty little catch out there," and everyone looked at Heidi and applauded, and Heidi smiled and turned red. It was the first time Biff had seen her embarrassed. He applauded and beamed, almost as if she were *his* catch.

CHAPTER SIXTEEN

It was raining on the island. Even though it was only one o'clock in the afternoon, most cars had their headlights on. Rolling off the ferry, they followed the Cha Cha bus for a mile or so, until it pulled into the parking lot of the famous seafood restaurant, Lulu's. Oh, those Cha Chas; they had all the fun. Maybe Heidi's father would take them to Lulu's for dinner. But the man lived in a trailer. A man who lives in a trailer probably wouldn't take them out to Lulu's. He probably ate squirrel for dinner or something.

"He does know you're bringing somebody," Biff said. "I called him this morning."

"Heidi, my sister told me your dad lives in a trailer."

"Yes, I suppose he does. So?"

"You, uh, failed to mention that."

"Did I?"

"What's he like, anyway?"

"You'll see."

"Can't you prepare me a little?"

"Oh, don't be nervous. Take a left up here where it veers off."

He put his blinker on and veered left. "I'm always nervous when I have to meet new people," he said. "I don't *like* new people. I only like old people. I hate having to make conversation. I suppose I'll have to make conversation with him. I like standing in a corner and observing. I'm a wallflower. A barnacle. I attach myself to submerged surfaces and then just observe the sea life. That's the way I like it."

"You are gibbering. Another left up here."

She led him farther and farther into the country, past farms, meadows, patches of forest, dilapidated barns and cottages. Occasional glimpses of the Sound reminded Biff they were on an island. He drove slowly, looking all around while trying to stay on the road. Fortunately, there wasn't much traffic.

Passing by a hilly pasture, he tooted his horn at the grazing sheep.

"This reminds me of England or Ireland or something," he said, suddenly lighthearted. "Or Scotland," he added.

"Ever been there?" she asked.

"Me? Nah. How about you?"

"Twice. Gran took me once when I was ten and once when I was thirteen. Gran's a real old-fashioned grandmother, the kind who takes her granddaughter to Europe for 'cultivating.' She's angry with me for refusing to have a 'coming-out party' on my sixteenth birthday. Can you believe it? It's the new thing in Spokane. My friend Fawn had one. At the tennis club. I swear, that silly dress she wore. God, you'd think it was her wedding gown. And her little bouquet of flowers. Ugh. But Gran. She's also mad because I insist on seeing my father. I told you she doesn't like me to visit him. You know what she did a while ago? She offered me money never to see him again, ever. She always did hate him. Take a right here."

He signaled, slowed down, and turned. "No kidding? She really tried to bribe you?"

"A few times."

"No offense, but were you tempted to take it?"

"No—yes—I don't know. She wants to run everybody's life. She wants to be God. She thinks she can buy whoever she wants."

"Was it a lot? Her bribe?"

"A nice round number. Four zeros. She actually wrote out a check and gave it to me, but didn't sign it. She said she'd sign it when I gave her my word I'd never see 'him' again. I carried the check around with me for a few days. I even carried it out on the train with me, the last time I came to visit him. I kept pulling it out and counting the zeros. And I kept asking myself: What's he ever done for me? And I told myself: If he's not there to pick me up at the station, I'll keep the check."

"But he showed up, huh?"

"No—well, eventually. He was two hours late. We had breakfast at Grig's that night—or morning."

"Did you tell him about the check?"

"Oh, no. He would've told me to take it. He would've insisted."

Biff shook his head. "Huh. She bribed you not to see your own father. What kind of a person would . . . ?" He shook his head again. "How'd you end up living with her for two years, anyway?"

Heidi was looking down at her hands, twisting one of her rings around and around. "The night my mother died, she and Gary drove over from Spokane. I stayed at the neighbor's while Dad went to the hospital. I really didn't know *what* was going on, just that something had happened. Gran comes walking in and says, 'My dear, Granny would like you to come stay with her for a while.' I didn't see my father until a few days later at the memorial service. I didn't see him again after that for four months. And that's how I ended up living with her. Two years later, Gran called me into her study and said, 'Dear, Granny's going on a fall-colors tour in New England. She would like you to stay with Gary and Sherri and Happy and Coco from now on. Won't that be nice?' It was no big deal to me, really, since Gary and Sherri only live a few houses from Gran. I saw them every day anyway, and I liked their house better than Gran's. Gary has a croquet course in his back yard."

"But you don't like living with them?" Biff asked.

"It's getting harder each year. For all of us. We're not easy to live with, though we do have our good points. Even Gary. He's basically good-hearted. And Sherri's a lot more pleasant drunk than sober. When she's sober she's very neurotic and bitchy. But we're definitely hard people to get along with. We're all kind of screwed up in our own way."

"Do you remember much about your mother?"

"Oh, yes. My mother was . . . she was a lot of things. I don't know . . . you never knew what mood she'd be in. But yes, I remember things. Picnics—Mom and Dad liked picnics. The Seafair Torchlight Parade. I saw a knife-fight there. I remember the three of us sitting around on New Year's Day watching the Huskies play in the Rose Bowl. I remember lots of things. I just don't think about it very much, that's all. Here's his driveway, on your left."

Biff turned up a long, narrow, muddy driveway riddled with ruts and lined on either side by bushes that scraped his car like fingernails. When they reached the end of the driveway, they came to a large mobile home with a dirty white Jeep Cherokee parked in front of it. To the right of the trailer was a grassy meadow; beyond that, woods. To the left was a small overgrown yard that stopped abruptly at a bluff overlooking Puget Sound.

"Hey, this isn't bad," Biff said.

"What did you expect?"

"Squalor."

There was a shed next to the jeep. On the roof of the shed was a black satellite dish for television reception.

They got out. Biff took a deep breath. He felt a light breeze that smelled of mountain meadows and rain and trees and wet sheep and sheep manure. And Puget Sound. He tried to ignore the satellite dish, but it was like trying to ignore a wart on the end of someone's nose.

"Deer come right up the driveway to the house," Heidi said.

"Trailer," he corrected.

"Whatever."

They both looked at the driveway, as if expecting a deer to come moseying around the corner.

"I wonder what the deer think of the satellite dish," Biff said.

"Shhh. Listen."

They listened.

"Quiet, isn't it," Heidi whispered.

She had a nice whisper.

"Quieter than quiet," Biff said. He liked that. "Quiet you can get in the city. But not quiet like this."

"Thank you, that was very profound."

He didn't want to go inside. He wanted to stay out here and look at the view from the bluff and explore the fields and woods and breathe the fresh air. It struck him as the kind of place he would have chosen for his hike. "Verdant." Yes. It seemed the perfect place to do some thinking.

But she took him by the hand and led him up the creaky steps of the trailer. He felt a slight tremor in his thighs at the feel of her soft, cool hand. Schmurr, he said to himself, you are definitely junior-high.

CHAPTER SEVENTEEN

He wondered if she'd knock on the aluminum trailer door or just walk in. She knocked. They stood waiting. The door opened. Heidi let go of his hand.

"Hi," she said.

"Hi."

Marc Hamilton had short, dark, neatly combed hair, graying at the temples. He needed a shave. He was wearing a light blue turtleneck sweater and dark blue slacks. He looked like he was dressed to play golf and then hang around the clubhouse afterward, sipping martinis and adding up his scorecard and talking about investments. He reminded Biff of a character in a book he'd read last summer. It was one of the most memorable and wonderful books Biff had ever read, but, as often happened, he couldn't remember the title, author, or name of the character. And yet, at the time he read it, he felt the book had enriched his life as nothing had for a long time. There was one scene in particular that stood out. The character is having dinner in a fancy restaurant in the South of France, and he notices Picasso sitting at another table. The great Picasso! No one else in the restaurant recognizes the grand old painter. The main character looks at Picasso once, and then averts his eyes, making up his mind that he's not going to stare, because Picasso simply looks like he's there to enjoy a quiet meal in a nice restaurant and doesn't need some guy gawking at him. Biff read that scene over and over. He kept thinking, That is *class*!

That was who Marc Hamilton reminded him of.

Mr. Hamilton looked at Biff, and then at Heidi, and smiled at her. It was a placid, fatherly, melancholy smile.

He held the door open for them as they came inside.

"Dad, this is Biff."

The handshake. The father's blue, cold eyes scrutinized Biff, and Biff got something he hadn't bargained for: the piercing glare of a father sizing up a boyfriend. Most unfair.

The trailer was warm inside, and once you were in it, you even felt as if you were in a house, though not a particularly solid one. But homey enough. There was a full pot of coffee in the kitchen, and the father poured them each a cup and offered them some milk, but no sugar. Biff wondered where the sugar was.

He left Heidi and her father in the kitchen and went into the living room. There wasn't much furniture, just a sofa, chair, floor lamp, coffee table, and TV. The TV looked brand-new, hi-tech, state-of-the-art, Japanese, expensive. The remote control on the coffee table was aimed toward the TV. And the satellite dish outside, aimed toward Mars.

Biff looked around the living room some more. There was a nice CD stereo system. And a stack of books piled up next to the sofa, and more books next to the floor lamp, which kept flickering on and off.

Heidi took charge, asking her father housekeeping questions, mostly about the status of grocery items and such. With paper and pencil she began taking inventory, going through the cupboards and refrigerator, making a list of groceries he needed, occasionally asking him where the so-and-so was she'd bought last month. At the same time, she was filling a large bucket with sudsy water. Biff couldn't help smiling at her sudden bustling efficiency.

"Dad, why don't you go in the living room and make conversation and I'll start tidying up in here," she said.

Uh-oh. The dreaded Make Conversation.

Mr. Hamilton strolled into the living room, where he and Biff stood and looked at a piece of butterscotch candy lying on the carpet. The father had his hands in the pockets of his slacks and jangled something—not keys or coins. What could it be?

"Have a seat, Biff."

"Well, you know, I think I might just stand for a while and stretch my uh . . . Feels good to—to stand after being in the uh . . . car and everything."

He and the father looked at the piece of butterscotch candy.

"Boy," Biff said. "Boy. That's a nice TV."

Mr. Hamilton nodded.

All right, your turn, Biff thought. I just said something.

"How about a beer, Biff?"

"Oh, no thanks, this coffee's . . ." Biff took a sip of the unsweetened coffee.

Marc Hamilton gave him a quick look, then nodded vaguely. "I believe I'll have one."

"Please do," Biff said. "I'll get it for you."

"You don't have to do that."

"No, I'd be glad to."

Biff went out to the kitchen, bumping his right pelvis into the sharp corner of the counter. Heidi smiled at him. "Out there." She pointed to the back porch.

He went out and found a large cooler, opened it, and looked at the array of different brands of beer, imported and domestic. He selected a domestic, because it had a twist top and wouldn't require hunting down a bottle opener—he was not good at finding things like that.

Back inside, he handed Marc Hamilton the beer. "Good place to keep beer out there, out on the uh . . . No use using the refrigerator when you can keep it just as cold out there on the uh . . ."

"Porch," the father said.

He thinks I'm a jerk, Biff thought. What should I call him, anyway? Mr. Hamilton? Sir? Marc? Hopefully, I won't have to call him anything. Heidi's not, after all, my girlfriend. I don't have to impress him. I'm not on display. Still, I'm not scoring very high on the first-impression meter.

"I just grabbed any brand," Biff said.

"You did well."

"You have an impressive array."

"Hm?"

"Of beer."

"Oh. Thank you."

"Dad, would you like a glass?" Heidi asked from the kitchen. She was busy making a lot of noise out there, but not too busy to monitor every word of their stimulating conversation.

"No. No, thanks."

"This sure is a nice place you have here," Biff said. He felt relieved, having reminded himself that this didn't really count, he was not a boyfriend subject to a father's approval. "Yeah," Biff said, nodding. "This is really a beautiful—a verdant area. Verdant is the word that sort of comes to mind. It reminds me of England or Ireland or something. Or Scotland. Real, uh, verdant."

"Yes," Mr. Hamilton said. "Pastoral."

"Pastoral!" Biff said, nodding. "That's a better word. Yes, pastoral. Sheep grazing and everything. Not that I've ever been over there—over there"—he pointed to Europe—"or anything. But I've, you know, seen pictures."

"Ah."

"Is all this—all that your property out there?" Biff asked.

"Yes."

"Sure is nice."

Mr. Hamilton smiled thinly.

Heidi called from the kitchen, "Dad, how long have those clothes been in the dryer? They look like they've been in there for days."

"Oh. Yes. I forgot."

"I'll just put it on air-dry and see if I can fluff them up a little."

"Oh . . . yes."

"And where are the vacuum-cleaner bags? I bought a whole box a couple of months ago."

"Oh, I . . ."

"Didn't I leave them in the closet?"

"Yes, I believe you must have," her father said, searching his pockets, as though the vacuum cleaner bags might be in one of them.

"Oh, here they are," Heidi said. "Never mind."

Carrying a new bag, she wheeled the vacuum cleaner into the living room.

"Hope you guys don't mind if I start vacuuming in a second." She bent down and picked up their focal point—the piece of butterscotch candy. "Dad," she said, "I see you've been using the vacuum cleaner, but you haven't replaced the bag, and it's way too full. You have to remember to replace it when it fills up."

"I . . . I see."

"Let me show you one more time how to replace this. It's not that hard. First, make sure it's unplugged."

"Yes, all right."

"Are you watching?"

"Yes. Yes, I'm watching. Go ahead."

Biff watched too. Heidi's white earrings dangled. She had her sleeves rolled up. Her numerous bracelets slid up and down her wrist. She explained each step to her father. She was quite good with the bag.

"Yes, I think I have it now," her father said.

"You sure?"

"Seems simple enough. Yes."

He had put his beer down on the coffee table. Heidi picked it up and took a sip and put it back down and went to plug in the vacuum cleaner.

The vacuum cleaner's whining seemed to make Mr. Hamilton uneasy. He picked up his beer. "Would you like to get some air, Bluff?"

"Pretty noisy in here, isn't it," Biff said. Had the father just called him Bluff?

"What?"

"Pretty noisy, isn't it!"

"Yes!"

They went outside. Biff left his coffee behind. Marc Hamilton carried his beer. He showed Biff around, but Biff knew he had just wanted to get away from the vacuum cleaner. Mr. Hamilton kept playing with something in his pocket. It was raining pleasantly, silently. They didn't say much.

Fifteen or twenty minutes passed. At one point Biff walked a few feet away. When he came back, Heidi's father was gone. He looked around, but there was no trace of him. He shrugged and went inside.

Heidi had finished vacuuming and was coiling the cord.

"Did your father come in here?" Biff asked.

"No. Did he disappear?"

"Yeah."

She looked away. Her lips parted and her eyebrows arched slightly. She had a smudge of dirt on the left side of her nose. "Probably went for a walk."

"Oh."

"I think he likes you, Biff."

"Really? How can you tell?"

"I can tell." Their eyes met momentarily.

She left him to entertain himself while she took a shower, and he looked around the trailer, which was now, thanks to her, neat and tidy. This trailer, at least what he'd seen of it so far, was a lot like his own room: impersonal. Nothing on the walls, nothing on the refrigerator either, except for a magnetic bottle opener. No photographs or coupons or phone numbers or personal memos or souvenirs; it was like one of those furniture showrooms—decorated but soulless.

Passing through the living room, he headed toward the two bedrooms and the bathroom, where he could hear the steady hiss of Heidi's shower. The spare bedroom on the right had nothing in it but a bed and a bookcase. He went to the other bedroom, tapped gently on the door to make sure no one was in there, glanced over his shoulder, and peeked in.

His eyes searched. For what? He wasn't sure. Something that would give him an idea of who Marc Hamilton was. And who Heidi was too, for that matter.

He saw a desk with nothing on it. Nothing. Not even a pencil holder or paperweight. Who ever heard of a desk with nothing on it?

He noticed a framed black-and-white photograph on top of the dresser and took a few steps closer. It was the profile of a woman, her head tipped back, looking up in kind of an artsy pose. The closer he came, the more of Heidi he could see in the face, especially around the eyes and cheekbones, and the large, defiant, "wild" mouth. She *was* beautiful and she *did* look like Sophia Loren.

His stare was broken by a *clunk* from the bathroom— Heidi must have dropped her soap in the tub—followed by the squeaking of faucet handles. He took one more look at Heidi's mother, then left.

CHAPTER EIGHTEEN

Heidi's father returned a half hour later. His eyes had a strange heaviness.

"Dad," Heidi said, "Biff and I'll go get your groceries. Could you give me some money?"

"Oh, yes . . . of course . . . but I don't . . ." He was searching his pockets. "My wallet, I . . ." He smiled apologetically. "Would anyone care for another beer?"

"I'll get you one," Biff said.

He went out to the back porch, glancing at his watch: 3:30. He was painfully hungry. It looked like they weren't going out for dinner, but at least they were going to the grocery store.

This time he selected an imported brand and was pleased with himself for remembering that he'd seen the bottle opener stuck to the refrigerator door. Back in the living room, Heidi's father had found his wallet and was pulling a plastic credit card from it. Biff handed him the bottle of beer along with the opener—Lynn Kobleska had once told him it was a sin to open another man's beer for him.

"Can we take your car, Dad?" Heidi asked. "I have my learner's permit but Biff won't let me drive his car because he's too cheap to buy the right kind of insurance."

"Of course." Her father gave Biff a wry smile and once more began searching his pockets. Meanwhile, Biff was remembering something else Lynn had told him, just last night: ". . . *like riding in the front seat of a death wagon.*"

"You're sure about this," Biff said as they walked out to her father's Jeep Cherokee.

"Sure about what?"

"You really want to drive?"

"Yes. You will observe my driving skills."

"It's raining. The roads are slick."

"So?"

"Heidi, I don't want to die."

"I'm so sure."

There comes a time when you have to face death, Biff thought. Who will mourn my passing? Besides my sister and father and, in her own distracted way, Mom, who'll probably think it's Wallace Jr. who's died all over again? There are worse things than death. Watching someone you love die. Being left-handed. Getting barbecued over a slow fire. Being forced to beg for your life—he'd die before he ever begged somebody for his life. Of course, that was easy to say . . .

They got in. Heidi started the engine, buckled up, adjusted the mirrors, adjusted her seat, then the mirrors some more, and then turned to Biff. A strange expression had come onto her face.

"What's wrong?" he asked.

"My father got high when he went for that walk. He smoked a joint and got fried. Is it obvious to you?"

"Now that you mention it."

Heidi looked out the window. She lifted her chin slightly and swallowed. "What do you think of my father, Biff?"

"Well, I don't know. I'll tell you the two words that come to mind. Gentle and class. Those are the two words."

"He is gentle, isn't he?" she said. "Biff, you know what?"

"What?"

"I like you."

He put his seat belt on.

Out on the road, there were few other cars on this rainy Sunday afternoon. Thank God.

"How am I doing so far?" She leaned forward stiffly, keeping her eyes straight ahead, both hands on the wheel, her chin raised.

"You might want to turn your headlights on."

"Ah, yes." She slowly reached down and flipped them on. In the passenger-side mirror, Biff saw a semi coming up behind them. Heidi kept looking at it in her rear-view mirror. Suddenly, she jerked the wheel and swerved over onto the gravel shoulder, barely slowing down, and the truck passed. Pretty soon another truck came from the other direction, toward them. Again she skidded over, kicking up gravel.

Biff tightened his seat belt.

"How, uh . . . ?"

"What?"

"How far?" he asked.

"The supermarket's about twenty miles. About five miles from the ferry terminal."

"On the way here, didn't I see a little store that said 'Bait and Tackle'?"

"Yes."

"Can't we go there?"

"No."

"Why not?"

"Why? Don't you like my driving?"

"Your driving is perfection itself. But uh"—he cleared his throat—"why go all that way?"

"Lots of reasons."

"Name two."

"One, I need the practice driving. Two, the Bait and Tackle shop—there it goes, by the way"—Biff watched it go by on the left and gave it a nod—"the Bait and Tackle shop doesn't have half the things I need. Three, the supermarket has a cash machine, which I am going to need to use, because my father gave me his cash card and his secret code. And four . . . what was four . . . oh yes. There's a pizza place near the supermarket, and you're going to order us a pizza for dinner, to go. I'll pay you back when I get the cash."

"That," said Biff, "is the best news I've heard since . . ."

"Since what, Biffo?"

Poor Biff was stumped for something witty and original. So he simply named his favorite food. "Since the invention of corn dogs."

"Oh, Biff, you're so weird, why do I like you? Do you say prayers at night?"

"No."

They drove on for a while. Biff looked at her a couple of times.

"Why?" he asked.

"Hm? No reason."

Biff rubbed his face. He looked out the window. Then back at Heidi. "You—you have to have a reason. You don't just go asking—"

"Shhhhhh. Don't get huffy while I'm driving."

He shook his head, clamped his teeth shut, and folded his arms.

The scenery rolled by.

After a while, she glanced at him. "It's just something my mother used to do with me, that's all. She'd come up and tuck me in—the nights she happened to be home—and lie on my bed and listen to me say my prayers. We'd talk, sometimes about God, sometimes about anything. And we'd hear my father in the next room, typing on his keyboard. It's just something I kind of miss. That's all."

She glanced at him, smiled, shrugged, and turned back to her driving, while Biff studied her profile, so much like the one he'd seen on Marc Hamilton's dresser.

CHAPTER NINETEEN

When they got to the parking lot, they split up. Heidi said she'd meet him back at the car. The pizza place was on the other side of the parking lot, and Biff left the car and walked over to it, glad to have his feet on solid ground.

The place was called Guide the Planet Pizza. What kind of name was that supposed to be? Heidi didn't know, and Biff found the name annoying; he was wary of any name with the word *planet* in it, fearing it might be one of those herbal all-natural vegetarian places that used ingredients like soybeans and whole-wheat crust and tofu. But Heidi had assured him it was good pizza.

The first thing he noticed when he walked in the place was the pair of pinball machines in the corner against the wall.

Thou shalt not go near.

With one glance he could see that there wasn't a single

customer in the place, yet a girl stood behind the counter with a big natural welcoming grin, ready for a sudden onrush of customers. Biff figured it had to be the nature of living near the ferry terminal: all that traffic coming in waves made you a little nutty. The girl was small and wiry: only her head, neck, and shoulders showed above the countertop.

"May I help you, Your Majesty?"

"Did you call me Your Majesty?" he asked.

"Sure did."

"Well, cut it out."

The girl laughed.

He named off the toppings that he and Heidi had agreed on and put his (or rather, Willa's) last twenty-dollar bill on the counter. When he saw the measly amount of change he got back—two bucks, a quarter, and two pennies—he clutched his heart and staggered.

The girl laughed again.

"Boy, that cleans me out," he said.

She laughed some more. What an audience.

"I'd like to know how this place got its name," he said.

"Yeah? Well, now"—she leaned forward, smiling into his eyes—"that's a long story."

"I've got time."

It wasn't a long story at all. Forty or fifty seconds was all it took. Maybe that was long for her. When she was finished, he was extremely sorry he had asked.

He walked around the place and looked at the photographs on the wall. Stan Crandall, March's Employee of the Month, was featured. There was a snapshot of an old fire engine. Why put a snapshot of an old fire engine on the wall of a pizza place? Things like that irritated him even more than the funky name.

Careful. He almost looked at the pinball machines. They were over there watching him. Instinctively, three fingers went to his pocket, pushed aside his two Teeny Bouncers, and felt the quarter he'd just been given. For some reason, Biff thought of Heidi's father, how the guy had snuck away for a few tokes, a quick high. What strange things we do to ourselves. Amusements, habits, obsessions.

His stomach growled. He looked over at the two pinball machines and licked his lips. One of the machines had been turned off, an *Out of Order* sign taped to it, but the other looked fit and healthy . . . and familiar. Ah yes. Pardy Hardy. An old nemesis. The picture on the machine showed fraternity men talking to big-busted sorority girls who looked more like *Playboy* bunnies than students. Maybe they were the Sorority Triplets of Gamma Gamma Delta.

The key to this machine was to resist aiming for the Extra Ball chute—certain death if you missed. Better to rack up points on the top bumpers and then go for the Double Value and Triple Value targets. It meant patient, methodical flipper work. And that Extra Ball chute was always a temptation.

He put the quarter in the slot and listened to it jingle its way down through the machine. The silver ball dropped into shooting position.

He pulled the lever back and let go.

His first two balls were not impressive, but on his third ball he had a clean shot at the Triple Value bull's-eye, which would have tripled his bonus points and given him enough for a free game. But he tensed up and missed. He was a bit rusty.

He hurried up to the counter and asked for a dollar's

worth of quarters and returned to the machine. The old fever. He played like a maniac. He used up all four quarters without winning a game.

He took out his wallet. One dollar left.

"How long before that pizza's ready?" he asked.

"Any second."

"I'll have four more quarters."

His forehead was wet. The girl, playing the role of bartender, nodded solemnly and put down four clean quarters. He took them to the machine, put one in, and left the other three on top of the machine and began playing.

"Pizza's ready," the girl said. "I'll leave it right here on the counter for you."

"Okay, thanks," Biff said over his shoulder.

He took his jacket off and laid it on the out-of-order machine and played on.

Finally, he had a hot ball and hit the bull's-eye at the right moment. *Plock.* Ah, holy noise!—he'd won a game. He kept the ball alive. *Plock.* Another game. What a rush, what a high!

Somehow he knew Heidi was standing behind him even before he heard her voice.

"I've been waiting in the car for fifteen minutes," she said.

"Sorry."

"I'm starving."

"I know. I can't help it. I'm sick. This is a sickness."

"Is that our pizza on the counter?"

"Uh, yeah."

He was still keeping the ball alive, but he trapped it for a second with his right flipper and turned around. "Heidi, let me finish this game."

She rolled her eyes and wandered over to look at the pictures of Stan Crandall and the fire engine.

Plock! . . . Plock!

"Whewee," the girl behind the counter said. "We got us a pinball weezard over here."

"Finished yet?" Heidi said.

He trapped the ball again. "Heidi, I've got four games. You play two and I'll play two. We'll kill them off. It's bad luck to walk away from a machine with free games on it, believe me."

"I will not touch that thing."

"Lemme just kill them off."

"Go ahead. I'm going. Bye."

He took his eyes off the ball for a second to see that she was walking out the door with the pizza.

"You can't leave without me," he said. "You've only got a learner's permit. No offense, but you shouldn't really be driving at all. Hey, I *paid* for that pizza!"

The door closed.

He finished the game, certain that she'd be outside waiting. Four games left on the machine, yet he managed to tear himself away and look out the window. He didn't see the car in the parking lot. He walked outside. It was raining lightly. He no longer felt hungry. The sweet *plock* echoed in his head.

She couldn't have left. No way. She wouldn't.

He hung around out front for a while. His hunger returned. He began to get panicky. She had to come back.

Another ten minutes passed. He went back inside.

"Howdy," the girl said.

He took out his wallet. The ferry tickets were in his car, which was at Marc Hamilton's trailer. His wallet was empty. All he had was a quarter, two pennies, and four games on the pinball machine. He went over to the pay phone and looked up Marc Hamilton's name in the phone book, but it wasn't there; he called Directory Assistance, but no listing of a Marc Hamilton. It was a twenty-mile walk. He wasn't even sure of the way. She couldn't have left him. She wouldn't be that cruel.

He continued playing pinball, but his heart wasn't in it. Thanks to *her.*

He finished off the remaining games, not caring how he did, glancing out the window every time he lost a ball. The girl behind the counter came over and watched him play.

"I'm in a little trouble," he told her.

"I noticed."

"I don't have my car."

"Oopsy."

"Don't say oopsy," he said.

"Okay, I won't."

"It's something *she'd* say."

"Sorry."

"That's all right. I guess I've got some walking to do."

"I could give you a lift when I get off," she said.

"What time do you get off?"

"Twelve-thirty."

He looked at his watch. "A mere six hours from now."

"Nuh-uh, five. It's Daylight Savings, 'member? Spring ahead, fall back?"

"Oh, yeah. Well, thanks for the offer."

He went outside and began to walk. It was raining and the sky was heavily clouded and he could hear rumbles of thunder in the distance, yet he could see patches of blue sky as well. Strange evening. The sun wouldn't be setting for another hour or so. He had his baseball cap in his pocket and he took it out and put it on. A car came by. He stuck out his thumb. The car slowed down, the driver leaned over and looked at him, and then sped up.

She'll come along, he thought. Where does she get off, ditching me? I'll strangle her. That's what I'll do. Provided I don't get strangled first, by some psycho driving around looking for hitchhikers—strangled and then dismembered and buried off some lousy logging road. What a way to die. But I won't beg. I'll fight to the end. But a logging road! They won't even find my remains for weeks, months, until the coyotes and small rodents have gnawed them to the bone. And all for what? Okay, maybe I went a little wild over the pinball. But she doesn't have to be so . . .

He shook his head. I wonder how far I've walked? Good tenth of a mile, maybe. Only nineteen and nine-tenths to go. What am I saying? She'll come along. If she hasn't driven into a ditch. Which would not surprise me. She'll deserve it, too.

He thought of the girl back in the pizza place. The way she'd smiled at him and kind of leaned toward him while she explained how Guide the Planet had gotten its name. "Life is like a pizza," she'd said. "You've got all these toppings and everything. Once in a blue moon, you get some combination that shouldn't taste good but it does and you wonder, 'What's behind it all? What's guiding it?' "

How ridiculous, Biff thought. Life wasn't like a pizza. Life was like a lot of things, but it wasn't like a pizza.

He took out his Teeny Bouncer and threw it up and caught it as he walked down the road. Life was weird, but occasionally it wasn't so bad. There were moments . . .

Another car whizzed by. In a hurry. More cars. A string of them. The ferry must have come in. He could see the pale, blank faces in each car. Would he have stopped for someone like himself? Good question. He's driving along and he sees this funny-looking poodle-haired kid walking: would he pick himself up? He had picked up two or three hitchhikers in his life. Any one of them might have slit his throat for the nickels in his pocket. He read about it every night over his two bowls of cereal. What a world. But what a world if nobody bothered to stop.

He quickened his pace.

And the rain came down harder.

CHAPTER TWENTY

He walked along the right-hand shoulder of the road at a steady clip, having reached a level of concentration where his mind was no longer aware of his body; nothing ached, groaned, creaked, or complained.

He believed he was on to something here. Concentration. Forgetting about Self. Listening to your thoughts. He walked faster, wishing he had a pencil and paper to write down some of his insights. How can you reach this level of concentration where you forget about your Self? Is that what death is? Is that what happens when you die? Where does your mind go when your body conks out? Is there just oblivion?

He looked up at the night sky. There were no answers. The sky had cleared; the rain had stopped a way back. There was no moon; he could see the stars. The Big Dipper to the northeast. And straight across to the northwest, the one that formed the letter M. Cassio something.

He wasn't entirely unconscious of his body. A pebble had found its way into his left shoe and every now and then he'd give his foot a little shake, without breaking stride, to reposition the pebble under his toes.

He had lost both Teeny Bouncers a few miles back. Search & Rescue aborted due to darkness.

No complaints, though. He felt fine. Past hunger. Funny how you get past it. Maybe it's like hypothermia. You get so cold you can't even feel it anymore. You lie down, get cozy, and die.

There he was, thinking about death again. It must have been because he'd visited Wallace Jr.'s grave today. Surely he could think of another subject. Here he was, after all, finally taking his twenty-mile hike. And not a single thought of Tommie.

Tommie . . . He tried to remember her breeze, her face, her voice when she'd come up to him last week in the hall. Last week—it seemed like last year! And all the weeks before that . . . Oblivion. And the months . . . All blended together. This was getting too weird for him. The time he'd spent with Heidi seemed one long day. How long had he known her, fifty hours? Twenty-three blurry months of being in love with Tommie, and only the past fifty hours seemed real.

What nerve Heidi had! Waltzing up to Tommie's front door and . . .

Biff laughed out loud. Leaving him stranded at a pizza place! And all because of a couple of games of pinball. That brat. Tommie would never . . .

"Praise Tommie!"

He bellowed the words into the night. Then he began to sing. He sang in a loud croaking desperate voice, accompanied by the *scrutch* of gravel, composing his backward poem in a gush of inspiration:

> *Slegn a nise veil eboh weimmot*
> *Won snig river up*
> *re hesi arp*
> *re hesi arp*
> *luo sym serot serehs*

Not bad! Yet . . . It didn't mean a whole lot to him anymore, backward or forward. His heart just wasn't in it.

Heidi . . . Why did pinball bother her so much? It didn't matter why. The point was that it did and he'd let her down.

He heard a car coming from behind. Its high beams lit up the dark road ahead of him. He moved far over to the ditch and continued crunching along the gravel.

The car passed, its brake lights flared, it slowed down, and stopped.

And backed up.

Uh-oh.

The driver leaned over and opened the passenger door. "Give ya ride?"

For an instant, Biff was like an animal—fight or flight. Yet he knew he wasn't going to turn and run, so he got in.

The driver could easily have passed for a psycho killer. Early twenties, long, stringy hair, a scruffy attempt at a beard. This beat-up old station wagon fit the part. Lynnyrd Skynnyrd's "Free Bird" was playing on the tape deck. Bad sign. Biff had read somewhere that Charles Manson types were usually into Lynnyrd Skynnyrd.

There was a dog in the back seat. The dog had a red bandana tied around its neck for a collar. That was a good sign: psycho killers usually weren't into tying bandanas around their dogs' necks.

Feeling a tongue on the back of his neck, Biff hoped it was the dog's.

He explained that he was looking for the left turn that led to the Bait and Tackle store. The driver nodded.

"Yeah, that's up here a ways. I'm Hank. That's Playboy in the back."

"I'm Biff."

"Playboy's been fartin' up a storm tonight."

"Really," said Biff.

"Musta been them Tater Tots."

They drove for a while without talking. Biff made sure his door was unlocked, just in case he had to dive out. "Free Bird" ended. Hank ejected the tape and looked over at Biff and Biff's eyes shifted left and right. Hank slowly brought the back of his hand up to his mouth and wiped it.

"Lotta rain lately."

"Boy," Biff said. "Boy. I got drenched back there."

"Turned into a nice night, though."

"Sure did," Biff said.

"Spring ain't far away."

"Baseball weather," Biff said.

"Haw?"

"Oh, I just said 'baseball weather.' "

Hank glared at him. "I knew that."

Biff glanced at Hank's face. Was that a twitch he saw, just below Hank's right eye?

"Lotta rain lately," Hank said again.

Biff cleared his throat. "Uh, yeah."

"Turned itself into a nice night, though."

Lordy, he's nuts. Biff felt for the door handle. Get ready . . .

"Go to many?" Hank asked.

"Uh . . . ?"

"Games," Hank said. "Baseball."

"Oh. Mariner games, yeah, I try to hit six or seven during the summer. How about you?"

"Me and Grandpa got season tickets."

Biff looked at him. "You what?"

"Got season tickets. Two rows above third-base dugout. We don't miss a game."

"You're kidding."

"Am not," Hank said, giving him a quick look.

"You really have season tickets?"

"Said I did."

Biff let go of the handle. "Wow. I mean that."

Hank nodded. "Pitchin' looks better'n ever."

"Uh, yeah," Biff said. He didn't really think it did, but he thought it best to agree with Hank at this point. "Who's that new kid they picked up in the college draft?"

"Peely."

"Peely, that's right," Biff said. "Sayron Peely."

"Left-hander, one-two-five ERA, senior year down at Oh-ree-gon State," Hank said. "Kid come outa nowhere. Got a fastball like a BB. Ain't gonna spend a single day in the Minors. We're just gonna have to see how old Say Peely does. Rookie pitcher in the Big Leagues, you never know."

"You never know," Biff agreed.

They talked about past Mariner teams and seasons.

Hank seemed very knowledgeable, so Biff decided to pose him the question that he and Ray Hu had been debating for two years: Who was the Mariners' all-time greatest third baseman? Hank's choice was different from both Biff's and Ray Hu's, but Hank backed it up with such solid statistical evidence that Biff actually found himself being swayed. This impressed him so much that he decided to ask him another question:

"Okay, Hank. Suppose you're a third baseman. A great fielding third baseman. And let's say, right in the middle of the season, you get hit by a truck and die. Where does all your ability go? Where does your third-base fielding ability go after you've gotten killed?"

Hank thought about this, stroking the wispy hairs on his chin. "Guess it'd have to get sealed up in the casket. Them things is air-tight."

"What if it's a cremation?"

"Haw?"

"What if they cremate you?"

"Well, then, it got burned up in the furnace. Don't know why you'd let yourself get cremated in the first place, though, when there's the Resurrection coming along and all that. Here's your turnoff. I got to let you go now."

Hank pulled over to the side of the road and stopped. Biff put his hand on the handle but hesitated.

"Take 'er easy, Hank."

"You take 'er easy yourself there, Biff."

He got out and watched Hank and Playboy drive away. "Take 'er easy," he repeated aloud. It gave him a good feeling. It had sounded surprisingly natural coming out of his mouth.

He started down the road saying, "Take 'er easy." A simple truth. Easier said than done.

What a weekend.

His legs now ached. He tried doing some yodeling to take his mind off his legs, but that made him think of pizza. He thought about the Mariners for a while, but they made him think of pizza too.

And then: headlights. A car came toward him, slowed down, and stopped. It was Heidi.

He climbed in the passenger side. "Got any pizza left?" he said.

"Lots. You mad?"

"Nah."

"I'm sorry, Biff."

"That's okay."

"I shouldn't have been so impatient."

"It was my fault. I thought I'd kicked the habit."

"You're really not mad?"

"It's hard to be mad after twenty miles."

She turned the jeep around, which took a long time because she had to be careful not to go into the ditch.

"At least you and your dad had some time together," he said. He glanced at her when she didn't respond. "While I was gone, I mean. You had some time together, right?"

"We had a good talk."

"Have you made up your mind?"

"Hm?"

"About whether you're going to live with him or not."

"Oh, we didn't really get into that. He does like you, by the way." She glanced at him and smiled. "He doesn't know why, but he does."

"I like him, too," Biff said. "Heidi, I like your father. I don't know why either, but I do."

Heidi emptied out the dryer and found one of her father's gray sweatshirts and gray sweatpants for Biff to wear while his own clothes dried out. Biff helped her fold the laundry, a job which usually gave him a stomachache but tonight was tolerable. His stomach did grumble while they were making the beds, but that was from hunger.

At last, he poured himself a Coke and sat down at a table off the living room and began gobbling his greasy, gooey Guide the Planet pizza. Heidi's father sat in the reclining chair in front of the TV and flipped through channels. Heidi finished putting another load of clothes into the washer, then sat down on the couch and put her bare feet on the coffee table.

Her father just stared at the TV, aiming the remote control and flipping nonstop through the million channels.

He's fried, Biff thought. Vegetonic.

They didn't talk much, just watched TV. Biff finished his pizza and took a bowl of strawberry ice cream over to the couch and sat down next to Heidi. The channel-flipping went on dizzyingly. Mr. Hamilton would land on each channel for anywhere from a few seconds to a full minute or two and then flip to the next. Occasionally, Heidi would say to her father, "Flip back for a second, Dad," and he'd flip back, and Heidi would maybe make a brief comment or not, and then, after a few seconds, he would flip on.

After about two hours of this, with Heidi and Biff squirming but staying put, Mr. Hamilton happened to land on one of the sports channels, where a boxing match was just beginning. He turned off the sound and turned on his stereo, for which he also had a remote control, so that he didn't have to move from his chair. Biff wondered if he was going to flip through the channels on the FM dial the same way he flipped through TV. But no, he kept it on a classical station and turned the volume up loud, and they watched boxing while listening to classical music. As soon as a round ended, her father would immediately start flipping through TV channels, but eventually end up back at the fight.

When one boxer finally knocked out the other, to the accompaniment of a four-horn concerto, Mr. Hamilton yawned, stood up, stretched, and announced that he was going to retire. As soon as he'd left the room, Heidi zapped the TV off, changed channels on the radio, and lit a cigarette.

"First one of the night," she said. "He doesn't like the smoke. It bothers his eyes."

"It bothers my eyes, too," Biff said.

Heidi smiled and blew a stream of smoke into his face. Biff reached out and tried to cover her mouth, but Heidi, laughing, fell back on the couch, and Biff dove on top of her. Three hours' pent-up TV-watching was suddenly unleashed. Heidi put her feet in his stomach and pushed him away, but he flung himself back on top of her and she kicked wildly. They fell on the floor.

Biff pinned her down and began tickling her armpit. She had hold of his hair. Suddenly Biff thought: This is just like the movies. These playful skirmishes always end in a passionate kiss, then the guy picks the girl up and carries her to the bedroom and rips her clothes off. The picking-up and carrying part I think I can manage—there's really not much meat on her bones. I even think

I can rip her clothes off. But the passionate kiss, that's going to be—

"Wait, time out," Heidi said, laughing and out of breath. "I've lost my ciga—oh my God, Biff, your hair's on fire!"

He found the cigarette and gave his hair a few quick pats. The smell was worse than anything else.

"Sorry," she said.

"No harm done. Tough way to lose a cigarette, though." He put the cigarette in his empty ice-cream dish.

"Let's play Scrabble," Heidi said, springing up off the floor and giving her hair a shake.

So much for the moment of passion. They spent the next half hour looking for the Scrabble game which Heidi had given her father two Christmases ago, but they couldn't find it. "It has to be around somewhere," she said. "He wouldn't have taken it anyplace." As a last resort, she tapped on her father's door and searched his room (while her father sat in bed reading), but, mysteriously, it never did turn up, so they went back to the couch and sat together with their feet on the coffee table and started reading their books—Heidi had picked up one of her father's—but ended up talking idly about nothing in particular, asking each other multiple-choice questions. (For instance, Heidi asked him which he'd rather be, a waiter, a pilot, or a truck driver; Biff chose truck driver.)

Heidi asked him why he was only going to community college next year and not to the university.

"I'll give you a choice of four answers," he said. "One: although I may seem brilliant, I actually only have a GPA of one-point-two. Two: lack of money. Three: my sister doesn't want me to move away. Four: absolutely no idea whatsoever."

"Hmm." She tapped her mouth with her index finger. "It couldn't be Three, because you could just commute. I doubt very much it's One. And it couldn't be Two, because you're smart enough to apply for financial aid, and besides that, your sister would pay for it. So I'll say Four."

"Bingo."

"I'm good at multiple choice, aren't I," she said. "Biff, how could you have no idea why you aren't going to the university?"

"Oh, it's not hard," he said. "Actually, I almost wasn't even going to go to community college."

"Why not?"

"Well, I was going to stay out a year or two and work in a self-service gas station my sister bought. It'd be a pretty good job, all I'd have to do is sit in a little glass booth and take money and keep resetting the pumps back to zero. I could have gotten a lot of reading done."

"Why don't you do it, then?"

"I decided it wouldn't be a good idea to spend that many hours a day looking at the world from inside a glass booth. I'm weird enough as it is."

They talked on into the early morning. Every so often, they'd open their books and start to read, until one of them started talking again.

Heidi left and came back with a blanket. They scrunched up closer together on the couch and got under it.

"You know, Heidi, I have to admit."

"What do you have to admit, Biff."

"I have to admit, at this moment life seems pretty good,

like one of those beer commercials. I'm pretty happy right now."

"So am I."

"Yeah?"

"Yes, but not like a beer commercial."

"Huh!" Biff shook his head. "You know, Heidi?"

"What?"

"I have to admit this would be a pretty nice place to live. If I were you—and this is just my opinion, of course—if I were you, I'd really think pretty seriously about moving in here. You know, you were talking that night we had breakfast at Grig's, about changing your life. Well, this would be a good start."

"Would it?"

"Much better than anything Richie Fitzpatrick could offer," he said. "That's just my opinion, of course."

"Can you reach my bag over there?" she asked.

He got hold of her bag and handed it to her. She took out her wallet and unzipped the money compartment. For a moment Biff thought she was finally going to pay him back for the cigarettes. What an odd time. But instead she took out a piece of paper and gave it to him. He unfolded it. It was a check, unsigned, for $10,000.

He let out a low whistle. "The old lady's bribe? You didn't tell me it still stands."

"It still stands."

"Why didn't you mention it earlier?"

"Because I didn't."

"Hm," he said. "It's a lot of money."

"It is a lot of money," she echoed. She put it back in her wallet and tossed her wallet on the coffee table.

"Well, Heidi, I'll give you my opinion again—not that

you asked for it. But here it is anyway. I think he's worth more than ten thousand bucks."

She gave him a smile, but it faltered. "It bothers me about that Scrabble game. He and I used to play all the time."

"What happened to him, Heidi? Why doesn't he write anymore?"

"He will someday. I'll get him going."

"Is it because your mom died?"

"She held him together. Hard to believe, but that's what she did. Biff, if I move here, will you come visit us?"

"Sure."

"Even though we don't do anything? Just sit around?"

"You bet."

"I'll still come and visit you, though," she said.

"Oh, sure. But I'd rather visit you here."

She yawned. "Biff, can I ask something of you?"

"You bet."

"It'll mean a lot to me."

"What?"

"Would you massage my feet?"

"Sure."

"I'm going to take my jeans off, because I don't need them on under this blanket. Do you think you can handle that?"

"I—ahem—think I can handle that."

"And if I fall asleep, just keep massaging my feet for as long as you want and then leave me here and you can go sleep in the guest room."

"I think I can handle that, too."

Heidi slid her jeans off and they rearranged themselves, so that she had her head down at one end of the sofa and her feet on his lap.

And Biff Schmurr began massaging her feet. He massaged not only with his hands but with his heart and soul, and after she'd fallen asleep, he continued massaging.

Looking up for a moment, he noticed that her wallet on the coffee table had fallen open to her picture of Richie Fitzpatrick. Richie was staring at Biff through his long blond bangs. Biff smiled.

CHAPTER
TWENTY-ONE

Biff woke up at dawn, on the couch, by himself. His whole body was stiff and sore—his legs from the twenty-mile hike, his neck from sleeping on the couch, his back from lifting Heidi up and carrying her into the guest room a few hours ago. He just wouldn't have felt right, leaving her on the couch.

His body was sore but his mind and senses felt more awake and alive than he'd ever known; his spirit felt noble. Ah, noble! Why? Because he'd carried a girl with no pants to the guest room? Well . . . It was a small beginning, but great things came from small beginnings. He even felt like whistling and singing, but he restrained himself. Instead, he went to the kitchen and made a pot of coffee.

It was Monday morning, the first official day of spring vacation.

While he waited for the coffee to gurgle and drip its way into the pot, he looked out the window and saw that the air was foggy and misty, but he knew that it would burn off and be a nice day. It was going to be a glorious day.

He looked around the kitchen for the sugar and finally found a five-pound bag of it in the bottom cupboard, but decided not to use any. A man in love does not need sugar in his coffee.

He put on his shoes and took his black coffee outside. The morning air was like a cold splash in the face. He stood and sipped the hot coffee. A solitary crow was cawing. He looked over at the driveway, hoping to see a deer, but the fog was too thick. He listened. He began to hear birds. All kinds of birds. The more he listened, the more different chirps and tweets he could distinguish. Ah, life! Ah, creaturedom. Was creaturedom a word? It should be.

He put his coffee cup down on the bottom step and walked out to the field, his tennis shoes brushing the wet grass. He stood still and held his breath. More birds. He inhaled. His legs, his body, had loosened up; he felt fine. His spirit soared.

He walked all the way across the field to the line of trees and plunged into the woods. Following a path, he came to a small pond, perfectly still. Mist was rising from it. Through the mist, on the other side of the pond, he saw a deer drinking. The deer raised its head and he and the deer looked at each other. Biff held himself as still as he could. Then he turned around and walked back to the trailer.

It was warm inside. He checked on Heidi; still asleep.

Her father emerged from his room.

"I made some coffee," Biff said and was pleased to see Mr. Hamilton pour himself a cup.

"Been outside already?" her father asked.

They talked about the weather, the field, the pond. It seemed easier to talk this morning, like they could have spent an hour talking if they'd wanted to. Well, maybe not an hour. Biff was glad the father didn't ask him about things like school or what his interests were or what he planned to do with his life. Pretty soon Mr. Hamilton said he was going out for his morning walk. Biff nodded.

He poured himself another cup of coffee, looked in again at Heidi, and went and sat down on the couch and read while he sipped his coffee. She could sleep all day if she wanted to. He'd wait for her.

When he opened his eyes, he found himself sprawled out on the couch, his mouth open, a trail of drool coming from the corner.

He sat up, wiping his mouth on his shoulder, and saw Heidi and her father sitting close together at the dining-room table, drinking coffee. Heidi was talking quietly to her father. Biff could just hear what she was saying.

"I'm thinking I might quit school."

"Oh?"

"I might get my GED. You know, it's the same as getting a diploma, it's this test you take, the equivalent of a diploma."

Mr. Hamilton nodded slowly.

"And then—I've done some checking up on this, you

see, Dad—there's another test, a more difficult test than the GED, you can take to get into community college. I'll—you see, I could maybe start community college this summer."

"Oh?"

"There's a community college right in Port Orchard," she said. "Not far from here at all. Just a ferry ride, really. I could live here and sort of take care of you, you know. And work part-time somewhere. I could keep the place in order and do the cooking. I wouldn't get in your way."

Her father was gazing at her, nodding absently, as if he heard her but didn't quite understand what language she was speaking.

The silence lasted a long time. Biff could see Heidi's hands on her lap under the table, twisting and twisting one of her silver rings. She glanced over at Biff and their eyes met.

Biff lay back on the couch and closed his eyes. His head was pounding so loud he could barely hear her next words.

"Say the word, Dad, and I'll move in."

"Well, I . . . What?"

"You need me. I can take care of you and stay out of your way. You can do some writing again. I'll help you get organized. You won't have to worry about household matters."

"Well, I . . ."

Another long silence, during which Biff stared at the ceiling so hard his eyes burned. He wanted to swallow, but couldn't.

"Well," Heidi said after a while, "we'd better be heading back."

"Oh . . . yes. I think that might be best," her father said in a low voice.

Biff heard them sipping their coffee.

"Goodbye, Biff," Mr. Hamilton said at the front door. "Come again."

"I'd like to," Biff said, but he wasn't smiling. They shook hands.

Marc Hamilton and his daughter embraced stiffly.

"See you in a couple months?" her father said.

"I might not be able to make it." Heidi wasn't looking at her father.

"Oh?"

"You see, the fact is, Dad, Gran doesn't feel I should see you anymore. She's sort of asked me not to."

"I see . . ." Her father was nodding.

"So it might be . . . it might be a long time."

"Ah, yes." He kept nodding.

"So goodbye, Dad."

"Well, yes, goodbye, then."

Heidi got in the car and crossed her arms.

Biff looked at her. "You want to drive?" he asked.

She shook her head.

"You all right?"

She nodded. Her eyes were moist. "He's so . . ."

She shut her eyes and raised her face slightly, as though feeling a breeze, and for a moment she looked calm and still. Then her face collapsed and tears came silently.

Biff fixed his eyes on the steering wheel. His hand shot up to the back of his head and scratched it. He put both hands on the wheel and gripped it hard. Heidi was sitting next to him, tears streaming. Comfort her, a voice told him. You blasted ninny. Can't you see . . . Where's all that noble love and compassion of yours? Here's your chance to put it to some practical use. Just reach out and comfort another human being . . .

But he could only gawk at the steering wheel, too embarrassed and self-conscious to look anywhere or make a move toward her.

Finally, he found the ignition with his key, started the car, and headed for the ferry and back to Seattle.

CHAPTER
TWENTY-TWO

That evening, Biff wandered around Willa's big, quiet house, carrying his *47 Secret Hikes* book, stopping occasionally to page through it. He didn't bother turning the lights on; the house grew darker, until he could no longer read the print.

Willa and Paul had left for the Oregon coast yesterday afternoon, after Paul had gotten off work at the supermarket, and wouldn't be back until Wednesday. Heidi and Pam were leaving early tomorrow morning for Vancouver, spending the first day there and the next in Victoria, returning Thursday. Even Ray Hu was gone: he and his family were skiing at Whistler Mountain. Biff felt pretty much alone.

He went to bed early, well before his midnight bowls of cereal. He glanced at the weather section in the paper and saw that tomorrow was predicted to be a typical April day in the Northwest: sun, wind, hail, thunder, lightning, rain. That narrowed it down, at least.

He set his alarm for sunrise, then on second thought set it an hour earlier.

He didn't sleep very well. His stomach woke him at one o'clock, growling "Cereal . . . cereal . . ." (It was still on Daylight Savings.) Shut up, he ordered. Back to sleep! But it persisted. *"I want my cereal."* He lay staring at the ceiling. He could hear the wind swishing the trees. He'd left his bathroom window open and his shower curtain was flapping. It knocked a bar of his Christmas tree soap into the tub, making a loud clatter similar to the one he'd heard yesterday while Heidi was in the shower. He wondered if she was awake right now. They'd hardly said a word during the long ride home from her father's, and now he wasn't sure they'd ever see each other again, or that she'd even want to talk to him, and he wouldn't blame her if she didn't. He had let her down yet again. Failed another test, the biggest test of all, the only one that mattered—giving of himself. Sure, if *he'd* been crying, he certainly wouldn't have wanted someone grabbing at him. But, oh boy, girls were different. They liked blubbering on somebody's shoulder.

The ferry took him across the Sound to the Olympic Peninsula, where he drove north toward Port Angeles. The hike he'd chosen—Deer Lake Trail Loop—was near the popular Hurricane Ridge Lodge, which had several heavily stomped trails. And that, according to his *47 Hikes* book, was why the Deer Lake Trail Loop was such a secret: everyone bypassed it in favor of the more glamorous Hurricane Ridge. The trailhead, unmarked, was practically hidden at the end of an old abandoned logging road. You had to use the map in the book to find it.

The morning was clear and sunny. The trail started out in thick timber, but after a mile or so, it opened up into alpine meadows, with sweeping views of Port Angeles, the Strait of Juan de Fuca, Victoria, the San Juans, and Mt. Baker. The slopes were covered with millions of blue and yellow wildflowers.

The sky began to cloud over with the blackest thunderheads Biff had ever seen, and before long, thunder boomed and lightning flashed and the rain came down in torrents. He sat on a rock under a tree, watching the downpour. Soon the storm passed, the sun came out, and a rainbow arched over the meadows. The beauty of it pierced his heart. He longed for someone, anyone, even a stranger, to share it with, but to share it with, well, someone like Heidi would have been bliss. He hadn't encountered a single human being during the entire hike, and he felt even more alone than he had last night, more alone than he'd ever felt in his life.

By the time he made it back to his car, he had devised a wild and bold scheme which involved driving to Port Angeles, crossing over the Strait to Victoria, and hunting down Heidi and Pam tomorrow. And then what? Well, tea and crumpets at the Empress. And then? That's where his plan sort of fizzled out. He didn't know what next. He realized it wasn't much of a plan.

He ended up simply driving home, exhausted. He fell into bed, slept solidly, and spent the next day, Wednesday, napping and eating and reading and puttering around the house.

And trying to come up with a new plan.

• • •

Willa came home around midnight, as Biff was sitting at the kitchen table with the Wednesday paper, halfheartedly eating a bowl of Cinnamon Toast Crunch. His sister was tired and grouchy. She and Paul had had one long argument from the Oregon coast to Seattle, and they'd ended up deciding maybe they'd better take a break from each other for a while. Biff wasn't surprised, but the news made him sad, and he pushed his cereal bowl away and put his head in his hands.

"Oh, Biffy," his sister said.

"No, it's not you guys."

"What is it, then?"

"Life."

"Poor Bippy. Go to bed."

He finally removed his hands from his face and looked at his sister. "Willa. There's something I need to ask you."

"Go ahead."

"It's kind of a favor."

"What is it, Bippy?"

"A major favor."

"What?"

"I don't want to ask it, Willa."

"Why not?"

"Because I already owe you too much. You're always doing things for me. I don't—I don't reciprocate. I don't do anything for anybody. I always pretend I'd do things for people, but when the opportunity comes up, I don't do it, and with you, the opportunity never comes up. What've I ever done for you, Willa? You're always giving and I'm always taking. The thing is, I don't even trust *myself,* I have no idea whether I really *would* do anything for you. It's easy to say I would, but . . ."

"You would, Biffy."

"You say that. But what you need is a brother, Willa. You need—"

"Oh, Biffy . . ."

"Wallace would have found plenty to do for you. Instead of taking from you and owing you. All I can hope is that someday, when the time comes, I won't let you down."

"I know you won't let me down. Now please tell me what the favor is, because I'm tired and I want to go to bed."

He hesitated. "I want to know if you'd let Heidi move in here for a while."

Willa's eyes expanded. "Oh!"

"It'd only be for a short time, probably. I haven't even asked her yet. It just came to me, just before you got home. She probably wouldn't be able to pay rent or anything, but she's good with housework-type things and cooking and changing vacuum-cleaner bags. It'd just be long enough for her to—"

"Of course she can, Biffy."

"Really?"

"Of course. She can stay as long as she wants. Is that all you were going to ask? Why don't you go to bed now. You look very tired. I'm going to bed."

"Willa?"

"Yes?"

"Thanks."

He sat at the kitchen table after she'd left. Then he put on his shoes and went out to his car. It felt good to get outside.

He found himself driving to Grig's. It was a little after one in the morning when he sat down in a booth. The same waitress as before brought him a menu along with his coffee. Without looking at the menu, he told her he'd just have a salad. "And make it the heart of the salad," he said. "I demand the heart of the salad."

"I'll see what I can do, honey." The waitress sauntered off.

There was a man sitting at the counter. Biff went up to him. "Can I bum a cigarette off you?"

Without looking at him, the man flipped out his pack. Biff took one. "Got a light?" Biff asked. He put the cigarette in his mouth while the man lit it.

"Thanks, mac," Biff said.

"Sure . . . mac." The man didn't look up from his newspaper.

Biff sat in the booth smoking without inhaling. He looked at his reflection in the window. A dork with a cigarette.

The waitress brought the salad and put it down in front of him. He looked down at the salad. Then up at the waitress. The waitress stood there with her hands on her hips.

"Honey, if that ain't the heart of the salad, I don't know what is. More coffee?"

The next day, Thursday, his spring vacation now three-fifths gone, he waited for Heidi and Pam to get home. Lynn wasn't home either, so Biff left three messages on Pam's answering machine.

He paced around, thinking how he was going to explain his plan to Heidi, and whether she'd go for it. Finally, about six o'clock, the phone rang and he picked it up on the first ring.

"Hello," he said.

"Hello. Is this Biff?"

It was a strange voice, a girl's. "Yes," he said.

"This is Tommie Isaac. How's your spring vacation going?"

He grabbed the table. The room lurched.

"Biff? Are you there?"

"Yes," he said. "I'm—going fine!"

"Good." She sounded rehearsed, as if she was reading her words from a script that she'd written out. "Biff, I was wondering, if you're not doing anything this Saturday, if you might like to go to this—this flute recital, at this art gallery in Henry Park, and afterward, after the recital, they're going to have espresso and baked items —baked items—baked items—such as—well, such as cookies, cakes, croissants, tortes, and—Would you like to go?"

He hadn't really heard what she'd said. He knew she'd ended with a simple yes or no question and a "yes" was all he needed to say. So he said it.

She seemed surprised. Then she began to tell him what time it was going to be and that she would be glad to drive, unless he had a problem with her driving, and she didn't mind if he *did* have a problem with her driving. If he did have a problem with it, he could drive, but she felt she ought to offer to drive since she was the one asking.

He was unable to follow what she was saying and he suspected *she* was unable to follow it, too. So he told her he had no problem with her driving.

She told him what time she'd come by and get him.

"Do you know where I live?" he asked.

She did. The address, she said, was in the phone book. "You're the only Schmurr in Seattle," she said.

"Yeah," he said. "There used to be a Gilbert Schmurr a couple of years ago, but he must have moved or something. You mean you looked my number up?"

"Yes."

"Oh."

"Why? Does that seem odd?"

"No, no. Uh, Tommie?"

"Yes?"

"This is going to sound strange, but did a girl come to your house last Saturday and, uh, mention me?"

"A girl? Um, no, not that I know of."

"Didn't a girl come to your house last Saturday?"

"I really don't think so. Was someone supposed to?"

"Well, no . . ."

"Oh, wait, someone *did* come to the house Saturday, now that you mention it. You're right, it was a girl. She said she was a sophomore, but I'd never seen her before. Do you know her?"

"Uh, yeah. I do."

"I guess she wasn't a burglar, then."

"A burglar?"

Tommie laughed. "The way she was kind of looking around, my dad thought maybe she was casing the joint, you know? He was just kidding, of course. But I don't understand. What was going on?"

"What did she say?"

"Oh, I don't know. She seemed a little confused. Just that she was So-and-so—I don't remember her name, Helen somebody—and she was a sophomore at Forest

Ridge, and she said she was on some committee—the Cookie Drive Committee, I think, and she said she was supposed to go around and ask some of the sophomore girls what their favorite cookies were, and I told her I'm not a sophomore, and she said, 'Oh, I'm sorry, you were on the list they gave me,' and I said that's okay, and she said I had a nice house, and then she left. Who was she, anyway?"

"Well, that's kind of a long story. Suppose I tell you on Saturday?"

"Okay. At least it'll give us something to talk about."

"Uh, Tommie?"

"Yes?"

"There's one slight problem."

"Oh?"

"I might be in Spokane on Saturday."

"Oh."

"In which case I—I wouldn't be able to go to the flute recital."

"No, I guess not . . ."

"I might have to drive that girl to Spokane."

"The girl who came to my house?"

"Yeah. She might be leaving tomorrow. She has a train ticket. She might go, but she might stay. If she goes, I think I'll have to give her a ride."

"Oh. I thought you said she has a train ticket?"

"Well, yes, but I think it would only be right for me to drive her back. Even if she decides to stay, I'd probably have to drive her over to Spokane to get her clothes and stuff."

"Is she your girlfriend, Biff?"

"What? Well, no. She's the niece of a friend of my sister's."

"Oh."

"I kind of had to show her around town. Well, I didn't *have* to. I mean, nobody forced me. But I showed her your house. Your house was one of the sights I showed her."

"Why did you show her my house?"

"Because she wanted to see it."

"Why?"

"Because . . . well, this is going to sound pretty ridiculous."

"Go ahead."

"Well, you know that essay I wrote? You said you kind of liked it?"

"Yes?"

"Well"—he wiped his forehead—"uh, Tommie?"

"Yes, Biff?"

"You know, on second thought, this is maybe something we should talk about after the flute recital."

"Okay. I guess we'll have plenty to talk about. Except, I think it sounds like you might be in Spokane on Saturday?"

"I really think I'd better hang up now."

"Okay, Biff."

"The thing is, Tommie, I'm kind of confused. I never expected you to call me, and it's caught me a little off-guard."

"I understand. Kind of. Well, let's see. Do you have my number? Why don't we just say you might come to the flute recital and you might not. Either way, I'll probably see you Monday at school, maybe. But if you can make it to the flute recital, then give me a call. If you can."

"I will."

"Well, goodbye then, Biff."

"Goodbye, Tommie."

He hung up. He stood with his eyes closed, wondering if you're supposed to wear a suit and tie to a flute recital. He'd have to ask Willa.

The phone rang again. He waited two rings, then picked it up.

"Biff? This is Tommie Isaac again."

"Oh, hi."

"Biff, I just wanted to say, I feel pretty good about that conversation we just had."

Biff closed his eyes and gripped the phone. "I do too, Tommie."

"Goodbye, Biff."

"Goodbye."

"Biff? I know you must think it's strange I called you like this. Right out of the blue. I was actually going to call you that day I talked to you in the hall. I've known about this flute recital for quite a while. I should have given you more notice."

"That's okay, Tommie."

They said goodbye again.

The phone rang. He picked it up on the first ring. It was Heidi.

"I'm back! I bet you were glad to be away from me for a while. I wasn't sure if you'd ever want to see me again. I brought you a present. Want to see it?"

"Yeah."

"Come on over. I'll be waiting."

C H A P T E R
T W E N T Y - T H R E E

It was shortly after seven o'clock on that clear Thursday evening when he met Heidi in front of the Kobleskas' condo. She was carrying a paper sack.

"Where shall we go?" he asked.

"Let's walk. It's a gorgeous evening."

They walked past the security gate and Biff started to turn left to walk along the Sound, but Heidi wanted to go right, to the Hiram Chittenden Locks. This was a grassy parklike area, right on the ship canal that connected saltwater Puget Sound with freshwater Lake Union.

They walked along the railroad tracks.

"Here," she said, handing him the sack. "This is for you."

"Oh. Thanks."

"It's not much, really. I bought it with the money I owe

you for the cigarettes, except I didn't even use all of two dollars. But I'll have you know I was up most of Tuesday night putting it together. See, I sort of assembled it myself."

He nodded. "I'm glad you told me that."

"Aren't you going to open it?"

"Do you want me to?"

"Of course."

"I will in a minute or two."

They walked on.

"You're disappointed in me, aren't you," she said, looking at him.

"Why would I be?"

"For telling you a big huge lie. About my father wanting me to . . ."

"Of course not," Biff said. "It's the other way around. I'm the one who let you down."

"I can't imagine how," she said.

"That morning we left your father's. You were crying. You needed my shoulder, is what you needed."

She laughed. "Biff, you are weird sometimes, but I like you. Have I told you that yet?"

"Which? That I'm weird or that you like me?"

They came to the park entrance. Several other people were out strolling.

"Will you ever see your father again?" Biff asked.

"I called him last night from Victoria."

"You did?"

"I have to keep seeing him. I don't know why, but I do. I told him I'd see him in two months."

"What about the check?"

"I tore it up."

"Really?"

"Don't you believe me?"

"I believe you," he said. "What about me? Will you visit me in two months?"

"Unless somebody pays me not to."

"Are you really leaving tomorrow?" he asked. "You don't have to leave tomorrow, you know. Listen, Tommie, I've been doing some thinking, and the way I see it, there are a few op—what's so funny?"

"You just called me Tommie."

"What?"

"You just called me Tommie."

"No, I didn't."

"Yes, you did. But go ahead. What options?"

"Okay, you don't have to leave. Now, this is something . . . we should sort of discuss this. Now, Willa has this huge house, see? All these empty rooms. You could come and live in one of the rooms, and if you didn't want to pay rent right away, you could just help with the housework or whatever. You could either enroll in school here, at Forest Ridge, or you could quit school altogether and get your GED and go on from there. But, now, Willa said it would be fine with her. For as long as you want. And the thing is, you see, it's not like you'd be living with *me* or anything. What do you think?"

She didn't answer. Her head was turned slightly, so he couldn't quite see her face.

"Well," he said, "it's not something you have to decide this minute. It's an option, that's all. It's always good to have an option. It's an option that you can use right now, or you can save it for later."

"It's nice of you to offer."

"I'm not trying to be nice," he said irritably. "I'm just trying to give you an option or two. I'm not trying to be

196

nice. All right, listen, I wasn't going to say this, but I'll say it. I want you to stay. I absolutely want you to stay."

She smiled and her body nudged his. They walked along in the deepening shadows. The breeze blew through the trees. They passed several couples strolling along the way.

"Why don't you open the sack now?" she said.

"I'm not ready to open the sack," he said.

"Don't get huffy," she said, smiling.

They walked on a little.

"Heidi?"

"Yes?"

"I'm ready to open the sack now."

"Good."

He reached inside and pulled out a plastic object that was the size of a teapot. It was a camel. One of the camel's legs had been cut off. A three-legged camel. The top of the camel's hump had been cut off too, and inside the hump, someone, presumably Heidi, had glued a glass ashtray, and at the bottom of the ashtray she had painted a set of bright red lips, puckered into kissing position.

"Heidi, I'm touched."

"I thought you would be."

"I'll cherish this for—for at least the rest of the weekend."

She smiled and linked her arm through his. It seemed to fit there naturally.

"I think, Biff . . ." Her voice sounded small.

"You think . . . ?"

"I think I might have to pass up your offer for now."

"That's not what I was hoping to hear," he said.

"Well, I'll tell you. You know, Pam and I did a lot of talking these past couple of days. We did a lot more talking than shopping, thank goodness. You know, sometimes she can come across as a bit scatterbrained, but I really do admire her. I have to admit she makes some good points, about finishing school and biting the bullet and all that. I think I'm going to bite the bullet and go back. And at least try to get along with everybody. But I reserve the option to take you up on your offer. And we can visit each other this summer."

"What about next year?"

"I don't know. I've got plenty of time. That's one thing I can count on. Lots of time."

They stood at the locks, watching the boats go through. The sun was setting and the wind had calmed. They walked on.

"Heidi, I'd like to drive you back tomorrow," he said. "You don't have to take the train. You can cash in your ticket. We can stop and see some sights along the way."

"It's six hours, Biff."

"I don't care. I want to drive you. In fact, I insist."

She stopped and removed her arm from his. She stood there with her eyes closed, as if she heard music. It was that 1960s flower-child look that he'd seen a few days back, at Brookdale Elementary.

She opened her eyes.

"You'd better think about it, Biff," she said. "You have no idea how awful it will be for you over there. Gary will want to take you wood chopping. He wants to take everybody wood chopping. Of course, you'll have to make conversation with them all—Gary, Sherri, Happy, Coco, and, most of all, my grandmother. She'll grill you. You don't know how she'll grill you, you poor boy."

"I can handle it."

"They'll make you stay for Sunday brunch. Gary will insist."

"I'll stay for Sunday brunch."

"That'll mean two nights. You can handle two nights?"

"Heidi, for you I can handle anything."

She stopped. Once again, barely smiling, she closed her eyes and lifted her face, and this time he got the message. He leaned toward her and kissed her.

She opened her eyes.

"Well?" she said, linking her arm through his as they started walking again.

"Well what?"

"Was it like licking an ashtray?"

"I don't know," he said, giving it some thought. "I've never licked one."